A Garden of Demons

BOOKS BY EDWARD HOWER

<u>Novels</u>

A Garden of Demons

Shadows and Elephants

Queen of the Silver Dollar

Night Train Blues

Wolf Tickets

The New Life Hotel

<u>Short Stories</u>

Voices in the Water

<u>Folklore</u>

The Pomegranate Princess and Other Tales from India

A
Garden
OF
Demons

Edward Hower

Ontario Review Press ✦ Princeton, NJ

Ontario Review Press
9 Honey Brook Drive
Princeton, NJ 08540

Distributed by W. W. Norton & Co.
500 Fifth Avenue
New York, NY 10110

Library of Congress Cataloging-in-Publication Data

Hower, Edward.
    A garden of demons / Edward Hower.—1st ed.
        p. cm.
    ISBN 0-86538-106-2 (alk. paper)
        1. Girls—Fiction. 2. Sri Lanka—Fiction. 3. Guerrillas—Fiction.
    4. Natural areas—Fiction. 5. Racially mixed children—Fiction.
    6. Americans—Sri Lanka—Fiction. I. Title.

    PS3558.O914 G37 2003
    813'.54—dc21
                                                                        2002066235

First Edition

For

Ivan Light

Christina Iovenko Howe

Michael Heinrich

Great friends

SRI LANKA

1998

"Can we open the gate, Papa—just a few inches?" Lila asked, and parted her fingers in the air to show what a tiny, innocent gap she was suggesting.

Derek, her father, looked up from his work on the garden path. "Sorry, *pol*, the gate has to stay closed." He called her *pol*—coconut—because, he'd said, her head was hard like one (the shell) but full of sweetness (the milk), and also because she had a way of crash-landing unexpectedly as if out of a tall tree.

"But what if he comes all this way from America and can't get in?"

"You'll hear him, then we can open it."

Lila tied two palm-frond mats together to form a slanting roof for her lean-to. "But I want to *see* him come!"

"We'll be seeing quite a lot of him, if history repeats."

"I hope so," Lila said.

Though the dawn air still smelled fresh and green, with whiffs of smoke drifting by from the plantation workers' cook-fires, the sun had already climbed to the top of a nearby hedge like a red-hot monkey. Beads of sweat glittered in Derek's bushy beard, and his blue shirt was damp from the heat. Lila watched him unwind a coil of silvery new barbed wire. He was making a trap for terrorists.

"You're not going to wait here all day, surely." Derek smiled. "You'll melt like a piece of toffee and turn into a sticky little puddle."

Lila laughed. "I won't!" Then she sighted at him through her fingers again.

Derek couldn't escape her gaze. Finally he clapped his hands loudly, twice. "Daya!"

Daya, the watchman, stepped smartly into the sunlight wearing a checked sarong, khaki shirt, and rubber beach sandals.

"You can unlock it, just for a short while," Derek told him.

The wrinkles on the old man's face bent into a frown. Pulling a key from the pouch strung around his neck, he slowly approached the gate's huge rusted padlock as if it were an oracle. Derek went back to the spiked wire coils, and Lila crawled into the lean-to. There, sitting on her sketch pad and colored pencils, was her orange cat, Zalie (short for "azalea"), who was already looking restless, about to creep away. For a moment, the cat let out the strange high-pitched mewing that often startled local people when they heard it rising like a wail out of tall weeds, as if from some invisible source. Lila's mother said Zalie made the strange noise because she was very old and a little cranky. Lila stroked the cat's neck until she seemed to smile; two tiny, sharp-pointed teeth appeared in the corners of her mouth.

The gate was made of solid steel and was painted bright green. On the outside was stenciled—in square black English letters and rounded Sinhala characters:

PRIVATE: NATURE SANCTUARY
Derek T.W. Gunasekera and Family

The gate was twice as tall as Daya, and as he tugged it partly open, it swung in with a groan, nearly knocking him backwards.

Now Lila could look down the shady tunnel made by the road and overhanging tree branches—all the way to the point of light where at any moment her Uncle Richard would arrive.

*

By mid-morning, the heat undulated along the ground, and the air vibrated with the buzz of insects from the jungle that bounded the plantation on three sides. As Lila lay belly-down on a blanket, sun-stripes leaked through the lean-to's slanting palm roof, making tiny fish-bone patterns on the back of her blue cotton dress. She was sketching an Air Lanka jet landing at the airport with two *yakkini*— benevolent spirits—perched like green, poppy-eyed parrots on each wing to guide the plane safely toward the terminal.

Toward noon, she dozed with one outstretched hand resting on her cat's tail. Zalie yawned, showing a sudden pink throat behind her teeth, then slunk off, body low to the ground.

A little later, Sue, Lila's mother, brought her a plate of coconut rice and pawpaw and some fresh bottled water. She was a thin, wiry American woman of thirty-five, whose caved-in cheeks and thick glasses gave her a tired and puzzled look, though she moved very quickly around the plantation and knew even more about its daily workings than Lila's father, who had been born in Sri Lanka. Sitting cross-legged before the lean-to in her long skirt and batik blouse, she reached out to feel the hair matting Lila's forehead. "You're soaked, dear!"

Lila sat up and rubbed her eyes. "I'm fine, Mum. Richard won't be much longer."

"You know, he must have had to catch a bus to the crossroads. The trip might be taking hours and hours." On Lila's last trip to Colombo, she remembered, vehicles were stopped at checkpoints for miles, passengers roasting in the

sun while soldiers demanded their papers and prodded
them with rifle butts. Lila still had a purple bruise on her
arm; though it didn't hurt any longer, she bit her lip in
anger whenever she noticed it. "Then he'd need to find a lift
all the way out here," Sue continued. "So why not come
into the house to wait for him?"

"I want to be here to meet him, just to make sure he's
okay," Lila said.

"Of course he will be."

"D'you think he'll be upset about the Land Rover?"

Sue sighed, glancing up the path to where Derek was still
working with the wire. "I wanted to drive to the airport to
meet Richard, too." She spoke to Lila in a hushed voice.
Then she smiled. "But he always finds his way, dear. And
he doesn't get upset about things anymore."

When Sue's brother had visited two years ago, and Lila
had been nine, everybody had to be careful not to say
things that might upset him. He seemed angry that he
hadn't found a job or a home in the States. Then the family
got him involved in a project to create a nature sanctuary,
planting flowers and trees everywhere. There were three
kinds of gardeners, Derek observed. Some saw works of
nature as lovely, colorful designs to be reproduced in art
(Lila—who rarely left the house without her sketch pad).
Others worked as if they were conducting scientific
experiments (Derek—who'd always wished he'd finished
his PhD in biology). And some treated nature as if
plants were innocent and vulnerable children (Richard—
and also Sue—who were re-creating their less-than-idyllic
childhoods).

Richard had worked in the sanctuary all day, returning to
the house covered in sweat and bug-bites but breathless
with reports of his accomplishments. Evenings were hard

for him, so Lila brought books into his room so they could read aloud to each other. Eventually they went through over a hundred books, including all twelve volumes of the illustrated Buddhist *Janaki* tales, with their delicious gore, magic, and noble deeds. She played cards with Richard every night for four months, too. He began to look better: his chopped hair grew out thick and curly; he was tanned and strong and much calmer.

But Lila thought he'd sounded upset in his last letter. Sue read it at the dinner table—"Can't you get Derek to find someone to fix that Land Rover!" he'd written. From the way her mother's voice emphasized Richard's question, Lila could picture him bearing down hard with his pen as he wrote. "It's insane to be stuck all the way out there without a car these days!" Reading over Sue's shoulder, her arms wrapped around her neck, Lila noticed the exclamation marks in the letter, and remembered that Richard had two of them shooting up in the middle of his forehead from the bridge of his nose. She used to run her fingertip along the indentations, trying to smooth them away. She loved the way he always let her, and sometimes it worked.

"My darlings, I'll see to the car absolutely as soon as I can," Derek promised Sue and Lila, smiling around the table.

But he was terribly busy these days. He had to patrol the grounds, to find workers to tap the rubber trees and harvest the coconuts. Especially he had to help put up wire security fences. There wasn't any extra cash to hire a mechanic for the car. He did get Hans, a neighbor, to look at it, but "the mad German," as Sue called him, was so drunk on locally brewed coconut toddy that he left the engine even more of a mess than he'd found it. Since then, the poor old car had huddled beside the house (a sick water buffalo, in Lila's drawing) with a tarpaulin over its snout. She had petted it this morning on her way down to the gate.

Now she looked up from her sketch of the airplane. "Mum, do you know why Richard's coming?"

"Just to see us, dear." Sue smiled.

"But any other reason?"

"Why should there be any?"

"I don't know...." Lila's voice trailed off.

Her mother was squinting up and down the garden path. "Where's Zalie?" she asked suddenly.

Lila squeezed her pencil. "Oops."

Sue's voice fell. "Oh, Lila! Don't you remember what your father said last time?"

She did. Her father had found a hummingbird lying on one of the paths, its wings iridescent as if it were alive but its head shiny with blood. Then he spotted the cat crouched in some weeds nearby. As soon as Zalie saw the look in his eyes, she sprang away as if scorched. Derek had walked over to Lila. "We live in a sanctuary," he reminded her, "and if the cat kills again"—he squatted down to hold Lila's cheeks gently in his cool, soft hands—"she'll have to be punished, won't she?"

"I'll look for Zalie," Lila told her mother now. "I don't want her to do anything bad."

"Especially not today." Sue stood up, cleaning her glasses on her blouse but just making them blurrier, Lila thought. "I want you to come to the house soon."

"All right." She watched her mother walk up the path, rubber sandals flapping at her heels.

*

Lila felt alone and impatient. Crawling out from her shelter, she climbed the plank steps to the guard-post behind the tall gate. A month ago her father had directed the workers to build an observation platform on wooden stilts. Now Daya spent much of the day up there on sentry duty in a sagging rattan chair. Lying across his lap was a rifle whose stock was attached to the barrel with rusted wire. Derek didn't allow guns on the plantation as a rule, but since Daya's didn't fire, he let the old man keep it.

"Daya, have you seen Zalie?" Lila asked in Sinhala.

He scratched his bald scalp. "No, Miss. But I am not on watch for pussycats. Only for Tigers."

Tamil Tigers were guerilla rebels who were fighting the government to get their own separate country in the north. "They aren't anywhere near here, it's only poachers we're keeping out," Lila said to Daya. This was what her parents had told her many times. They'd also said that since the Tigers were Hindus—Tamil people originally from South India—and the government was mostly Buddhist—run by Sinhalese people who'd come from North India centuries ago—her family was considered neutral. Her father's people, though Sinhalese, had nominally converted to Christianity during the British colonial era, and most people assumed that Lila's mother, being a foreigner, was a Christian, too (though in fact she'd been studying Buddhism before leaving America). "Besides, everybody knows the plantation's a nature sanctuary, a neutral place," Lila continued. "There's nothing here to interest any guerillas."

"Your father told you this," Daya said. "He believes in the sanctuary."

"What—don't you?"

Daya's jaw worked up and down as if he were chewing on the question. "I think it is a fine and beautiful idea," he said finally, "but the plantation should be pegged, just in case."

Many people hammered wooden pegs into the ground around the boundaries of their property to keep bad demons away. Lila had never actually seen a demon—as far as she knew (they could take human or animal shapes)—but she'd often heard them, and she had sensed their presence in and around the house all her life. But she didn't believe, as Daya and the workers apparently did, that Zalie was sometimes possessed by a demon that wanted to bring trouble onto the plantation. Sometimes she worried that her father believed this, too, though he denied it. As a child, he'd seen plenty of demons, of course, good and bad— "bald and hairy ones, fat and skeletal ones, fanged and toothless ones," as he reported, shaping them in the air with both hands. Nowadays, though, he only occasionally glimpsed one out of the corner of his eye, he said, and even then it might just be a sunspot or the shadow of a flying fruit bat. Lila's mother, over the years, had come to accept demons, the way she did the termites that invisibly ate the door frames and the mysterious head-pains that sometimes knocked Derek nearly senseless for days and nights on end.

"What good are pegs against Tigers?" Lila asked Daya. "Tigers are humans, not demons."

"Tiger terrorists are worse." Daya spat a stream of betel juice from the platform onto the dust below. "They are Tamils."

"No—most Tamils aren't Tigers," Lila insisted, frowning. She had several Tamil friends whose families had worked on the plantation for generations. Radha, her best friend at school, was the daughter of a Tamil doctor and nurse who ran the crossroads clinic.

"If you say so, Miss," Daya said. "I am sure there is nothing for us to worry about."

"Well…yes, there is." Lila lowered her voice, glancing around. "Zalie's gone missing. Will you help me find her?"

"Of course." Daya pulled a canvas bag onto his lap. He took out a yellow cellular phone, pretended to switch it on, and called into its plastic mouthpiece, "Zalie! Come in, Zalie!" He grinned, showing gaps between his teeth. His betel-chewing habit had turned them dark red. "Over and out."

Lila tried not to smile, but she couldn't help herself. She pointed to the canvas bag. "May I have the glasses, please?" she asked.

"Yes, yes." Daya pulled out a pair of binoculars and handed them to her.

They were heavy, and Lila had to adjust them to her small face, but she managed them expertly, twisting the eyepiece rings to bring the landscape into focus. Now she felt as if she were soaring over the countryside like a crow in one of her paintings. First she flew up the rutted dirt driveway lined by the trees her father and Richard had planted two years before. Then she hovered over the front garden. White, purple, and red spots flicked up at her— flowers in every shape and size: trumpets and balls and plumes…but no plump orange cat. Veering right, she flew over the sanctuary area, which took up most of the plantation now. Lila swooped low over old vine-covered arbors that tilted like wrecked galleons festooned with sea-weeds. Where the land had been reclaimed, some paths were lined with barbed wire. Circles of whitewashed stones surrounded cement fountains where, as yet, no water spouted. More rows of trees wore wooden labels tied around their trunks like shiny bow ties. Near the gate was the false path her father had been working on all morning.

Anyone running along it would get trapped between two gradually narrowing barbed-wire fences; the more the intruder thrashed, the tighter he'd be caught.

Hearing the rumble of an approaching engine—Richard, finally?—she raised the binoculars to swoop along the road beyond the gate. Out of the tunnel of tree branches appeared a new but battered red Jeep, its bumper smashed sideways so that the car tilted at a rakish angle. It belonged to a neighbor, Hans the German. His yellow hair streamed behind him; his girlfriend clung to his side like a scared beetle. Lila pressed her hands to her ears as he swerved past.

A Tamil woman in a sari turned away from the Jeep's swirling dust cloud. A Sinhalese woman in a bodice and cotton skirt joined her on the roadside. Soon Lila would wear a grown-up outfit like this woman's; only little girls—and Christians—wore Western dresses. Except for the clothes these women had on, you couldn't tell that they were of different religions or ethnic groups—both were equally dark-skinned, graceful, and muscular.

Lila herself was almost as dark as her father—"a throwback to my royal ancestors," he said. Her skin was "the lovely color of fresh cinnamon," Sue said. And her hair was "as smooth as black silk." After Sue washed it, she and Derek would sit in the garden with Lila, taking turns with the towel and brush—"making you shine," they said. From the side, Lila looked much like her schoolmates, small and lithe, but as soon as she faced anyone with wide-open eyes—as she sometimes did to stare down girls who said nasty things to her—she looked different from everyone in the world. Her eyes were a purply-blue and glowed out of her dark face in such a way that some adults shielded their children from her gaze. Once she'd asked her parents if she had the evil eye.

"Certainly not!" Sue said. "You've got the softest, most benign eyes of any of nature's creatures."

Derek gazed at her. "Like *sambhurs'*." He knew that they—wild deer—were Lila's favorite animals, though of course their eyes weren't blue. Nobody in her family had blue eyes except Richard. "And," Sue said, thrilling her, "your great grandmother." She'd been a beautiful frontier woman who'd tamed wild horses and started her own school and lived to be ninety-nine.

At 3:20 by Lila's red plastic watch, she heard the creak of wooden wheels. A bullock cart came into view: the animal plodding along, the driver dozing behind. The cart—when it was equipped with seats and a canvas roof—took Lila and other girls to and from school at the crossroads. As many as twenty girls squashed in together in their uniforms, plaiting each other's hair and chirping "like an aviary on wheels," as Lila's mother described the sound they made. School was closed for the holidays now, so the driver was transporting sacks of rice instead of students. Lila hoped Richard wouldn't arrive in a cart; she wanted him to get down from a big shiny taxi sedan, or at least one of the black and yellow three-wheeled scooter-taxis that swarmed like hornets around the crossroads market.

Pacing the observation platform, she scanned both sides of the fence. No cat on the right side of it in the plantation. No Richard to her left side, on the road. But out of its shady canopy of branches came a harsh, metallic clunking sound: two men riding on a wobbly black bicycle. The poor man who sat sideways on the back wore a filthy bandage around the stump of his leg where his foot should have been. The stump hung limp in the air beneath him. He blurred in the binoculars as he came closer; Lila dropped the glasses from her face, and he grew sharper than before: young, dark-haired, with big, sad eyes. Raising one hand to his forehead, he gave Lila a silent salute, as if he knew her.

And suddenly it seemed to Lila that he *did* know her, and that she knew him. She'd seen war-wounded men before, but none had ever saluted her like this. Feeling awkward, standing high above the man, she waved slowly at him. She waved till her arm ached. Then he was gone and the road was empty again. The bicycle's clatter was gone. Lila's eyes stung with sweat. She wiped them with her fingers. The emptiness the man left behind made a vibration in the air that seemed to rise up from the land around her—a kind of sound more insistent than the buzz of insects or the hissing of rain at night or gusts of wind crackling in the palm fronds. But when she leaned forward to listen to what it might be saying—it rushed away from her.

She knew that she would draw the sound: a dark ocean of flames spilling across the plain, with high waves and sea monsters splashing, snarling, snapping—a disturbing scene, but *hers*. Now in her mind she saw the fiery water flow along the paddy fields and wash over the green hills in the distance: waiting there, ready to rush back another time. She was left stranded on the platform with her sweat-drenched dress stuck to her chest and back.

Then, at the same moment, two things happened.

To her right, she saw Zalie burst out of a cluster of flowers, running with quick, dainty steps up the path toward Derek. Clamped in her teeth was something raw, pink, fluffy-tailed...and dead: a baby squirrel.

"Zalie, *no!*" Lila screamed.

And to her left, she saw an old blue taxi approaching along the road. It screeched to a halt outside the gate. Down the platform's rickety steps she ran.

Years later, she would wonder what might have happened if she'd chased Zalie into the bushes out of sight before her father had spotted the squirrel in the cat's mouth. But now she clutched the edge of the heavy steel gate beside Daya and tugged until it swung all the way back. The taxi wobbled toward her over the driveway's ruts. Its door swung open wide. A familiar figure leaned out from the back seat.

"Uncle Richard!" She flung herself blindly into the car, sure that he would catch her.

TWO

"Lila—watch out!"

Richard pulled her back as the car tilted on two wheels, then righted itself with a bounce. Laughing, Lila held tight to her uncle's arm. Fence posts swished past outside. The driver, a man with a knitted Moslem cap, halted the taxi in front of the house. Richard relaxed his grip, and Lila squirmed around to peer into his face.

"You came! You're back!" she said, out of breath. "Are you okay now?"

"Sure, I am!" He grinned, and his shaggy red-brown mustache—he'd grown it here last time—jumped up at the corners. His eyes were as blue and crinkly as before. "And you—you've grown so much!"

Lila, still the smallest girl in her class, beamed. Then Richard's door swung open and Sue was tugging him out of the car. She threw her arms around him as he stood, digging her fingertips into his back and shutting her eyes tight against his shoulder.

"Suzy!" Hugging her back, he sounded as if the air were rushing out of him.

Sue laughed aloud. They stood apart to gaze at each other, her eyes damp. Lila wriggled between them. Holding her hand, Richard walked into the front yard, stretching his legs and staring up at the house. Around the old stone walls leaned tall bushes drooping with horn-flowers (in one of Lila's drawings, they were trumpets tooting pastel streaks). A canopy of leafy tree branches formed a second roof resting on the mossy tiles; vines twisted along them (snakes fallen asleep while wrestling). The windows with their dark metal security bars were thrown open now, but the house still seemed to have trouble peering out of all the beautiful foliage. Lila often drew Zalie framed in a window-eye like its pupil; the cat wasn't there now, though. Richard took a long look at the Land Rover buried under its black tarpaulin; vines were starting to grow over it already. She tugged him back toward the front steps.

Sue was waiting there. "Wouldn't you like some tea?"

Richard smiled. In America, Lila knew, people didn't have afternoon tea, but Richard said, "I'd love it."

"Derek should be here." Sue glanced around. "Though you never know with him."

"How *is* he?"

"You never know."

"Papa was on the driveway when Richard came," Lila said. And then, as if brought to life by her voice, he appeared, striding up the hill toward Richard.

"Welcome, brother!" he said, his teeth flashing white in his beard. He'd often called Richard "brother" last time in the same cordial voice, but now he didn't hug him, just shook hands with him. "Not too jet-lagged? No, you look fine. Come inside out of the heat—come—"

Before tea, Richard had a wash. "Sorry we don't have a real shower yet," Sue said, just as Lila remembered her saying two years ago. He squatted in the outdoor laundry room beside the tap in his undershorts while Sue and Lila soaped his back and poured buckets-full of cold water over him. His back was light brown and rippled with muscles. When he stood up, his hair dripped down to his shoulders. *"Ahh,"* he kept saying, letting out long deep breaths that seemed part laughs, part gasps.

While Richard was in his room dressing, Lila lay down on one of the living room sofas to wait for him. She could smell the lovely fresh soap scent coming from his room. In the kitchen, Sue cranked the coconut grinder—but slowly and quietly so as not to disturb Derek, who was having head-pains again lately. Was he blaming Zalie for them? Lila wondered. She'd never seen him harm any living creature, even the scorpions that scuttled up from under the rubber-smoking shed or the ribbon-like green cobras that lived in the garden stump. Still, she'd been keeping the cat in her room while her father was nearby. There was no telling where he might be now. Or Zalie either.

The coconut-scraping sound stopped; now she could hear the overhead fan whirring slowly in the rafters above her. The house had its own faintly creaking sound in the late afternoon, as if gently squeezing out the light and hot air to get ready for sunset. She'd never noticed this before; perhaps it was because Richard was here. Things already seemed different in the house. When Derek's father had bought it long before Lila was born, she remembered her father telling Richard, it was called a "planter's bunga-low"—this was during colonial times—though the seller wasn't a Briton but a Sinhalese family that had owned the plantation since the last century. The old furniture in the long central room had come from big houses, many of them sold now, that Derek's family had owned near Colombo. To the left of the sofa where Lila lay was Sue and Derek's bedroom and an office where stacks of blueprints were held down by an elderly black typewriter; to her right was a guest room, never used since Richard's last visit, and a bathroom, and Lila's bedroom. The kitchen and laundry room were connected to the house by short corridors off the dining area.

From the windows flapped long faded red curtains (tongues of huge lizards outdoors trying to lick crumbs off the tables inside). The room was lined with bookshelves

holding hundreds of books in cases from floor to ceiling—
all the texts that Derek and Sue had collected during their
years at the American university where they'd met. Lila
had been reading the books since she'd been big enough to
balance them on her knees. She'd pored over Derek's
biology texts; redwood trees and orange azalea bushes
were nearly as familiar to her as the tropical flora outdoors.
She also loved Sue's big Art History texts and her
collections of 1960s rock music posters with curly letters
that turned into long-haired ladies and bearded guitar
players. Best were the illustrated Eastern Religion books.
She liked the monkey-faced Hindu deity who flew through
the sky trailing a flaming tail, and a voluptuous, dark-
skinned, six-armed goddess who decapitated whole demon
armies with her blood-spraying swords. Lila was fond of
the tubby Hindu elephant-headed god, Ganesh, too, and
had painted him sitting in the Sprite Tea Shop down the
road, eating sweets with his friend the mouse. But of course
she loved the Buddha best, and Sri Lanka's special spirits,
gods, and demons, both beneficent and wicked. She
painted a lot of Buddhas, in male, female, and animal
incarnations. In one picture he wore white slacks and a
cable-knit sweater: a smiling umpire at a game of cricket
she and her parents were shown playing beneath the big
gum tree in the front yard.

Finally Richard came out of his room wearing a maroon
sarong Sue and Lila had chosen for him at the crossroads
market last week. His hair was tied back with an elastic
band; he didn't look as huge as Lila remembered him, but
tanner and stronger. He was thirty now, five years younger
than Sue and Derek. To Lila he'd appeared much younger
than them last time—almost a teenager—but now he
seemed the same age they were, if not older, somehow.

"Come on," Lila whispered, pulling him by the hand to the two sofas. On the coffee table between them she'd set out the black leather artist's portfolio Richard had mailed her from America. (She hadn't known what a portfolio was until she'd opened the package, hadn't even known she was an "artist.") The big string-bound book was fat with 197 paintings now: oils and pastels and watercolors, as well as pencil and crayon sketches. This didn't count the fourteen pictures her parents had framed and hung all over the house.

Lila opened the portfolio. On the first page was a painting of Zalie, but Lila didn't feel like looking at the cat right now and flipped ahead to pictures of a *sambhur* deer, some orchids and bougainvillea, portraits of her mother, her father, the country's prime minister in a red sari, and a flock of Christian angels. Richard kept saying "Amazing! Terrific!" so Lila didn't rush through the book. She'd be glad if it would last for months.

"Remember this?" Lila asked, turning to a painting of a long, green monitor lizard lumbering out of a steamy bog. These dog-sized lizards were as harmless and as common here as geckos, but to Lila they'd seemed mysterious ever since Richard had been spooked by one.

"Oh, yeah," he grinned. "The first time we saw one, I thought it was a dinosaur."

"That's why it came out like that." Lila pointed to huge prehistoric-looking ferns looming around the swamp. A long-beaked pterodactyl streaked across the sky.

"You didn't plan it?" Richard looked at her.

"No. Sometimes the pictures just come into my head and I have to let them out. But sometimes they're already on the paper and I just fill them in." Lila shrugged and turned a page. "I didn't draw this one, though."

The paper was covered with tiny red-inked hands. Radha, Lila's Tamil friend, had brought her back a rubber stamp from a holiday in India, she told Richard. People there dipped their hands in dye and slapped their palms against walls—the print was supposed to keep away the evil eye. Lila had stamped little hands all over the house; they came off easily with a wet cloth, but Sue and Derek had left them alone until they faded.

A much better way to keep safe from bad influences, Sue said, was to celebrate *Vesak*, the Buddha's birthday, inviting good wishes on the house. This year, the holiday had come just a few days before Richard's arrival, and the decorations were still up. Lila pointed out the strips of paper she and her mother had hung from the rafters. Crayoned in bright Buddhist colors, they flapped and swung in the fan's breeze.

Richard lay on the sofa so he could stare straight up at the papers. From one end of the room to the other they fluttered in a dance of perpetual happiness. "Look at them all!" he said, smiling. "It's an indoor carnival."

"There's dozens," Lila said. "It took us two weeks to make them."

"They sound as if they're whispering."

"That's the prayers we wrote on the papers, Mum says."

"Right." Richard closed his eyes as if to listen more closely.

Lila watched him. Maybe he was too tired to look at more pictures now. "Do you want to play rummy?" she asked. "You're still ahead."

"What, from last time?" Richard blinked open his eyes and gazed at the notebook she handed him. On the day he'd left—March 5, 1996—he was leading in rummy 3,321 points to 2,995; she was winning Go Fish 121 games to 99.

"It's like I've just stepped out of the room for a second and come back," he said.

"Shall I deal?" Lila asked.

But then Sue appeared with a big tray. "Tea," she said, setting it down on the table.

Lila groaned, leaning her forehead against Richard's arm. "Rummy after tea?"

"Right after tea." Richard ruffled her hair.

The front door opened. Derek, who often went away quietly without saying where he was going and came back without any news of where he'd been, appeared with four golden-brown mangoes, two in each hand. "They're perfect—the season's just starting," he said to Richard, and went into the kitchen to wash them.

Tea was very long; eventually it blended strangely into supper, which was like having dessert before the meal and then after it again. Sue had baked a cake as best she could with the oven not working very well.

"Rats get into its wiring," Derek explained to Richard. "They chew off the insulation—"

"—So you can never tell exactly what the oven temperature's going to be," Sue finished.

Richard asked if they set traps, but Derek and Sue shook their heads in unison.

Lila knelt on her chair to whisper in Richard's ear. "No killing of creatures allowed here."

"More would come back, anyway," Sue said.

"The estate was a jungle when my father bought it," Derek said.

Sue nodded. "And the minute you turn your back, it tries to turn into jungle again."

"My father knew the name of every worker on the place," Derek said.

"There must have been twenty families, weren't there?" Sue asked.

"At least." Derek finished his cake. White crumbs speckled his black beard. "They've been here for generations—in little compounds inside and outside the fence. They keep the place cleared, harvest the coconuts, tap the rubber trees, plow the vegetable gardens, tend the paddy fields—all for a share, of course, and wages, some of them."

Sue stared down into her teacup. "Nowadays strangers are moving onto the place. Sometimes we hardly know who's living out there any longer—"

"New families are here now, it's true, but still—" Derek turned to Richard. "—they're good people, Sinhalese and Tamil both. We all get along here."

"Oh, that's true." Sue looked up quickly and smiled.

Lila had stopped listening after the mention of the jungle, where she was forbidden to go alone, though she often did slink through its underbrush looking for *sambhurs* and other animals. "There were monkeys on the roof last week," she said, her mouth full of mango. "They were *mating!*" Juice dribbled out the side of her mouth. "Daya said so. It's the season."

"Like the mangoes?" Richard asked.

"Mangoes don't mate!" Lila buried her face in her napkin.

"The monkeys were screeching and jumping around," Sue said.

"We all went outdoors with flashlights and threw coconut husks at them," Derek said.

"They threw them back down at us," Lila said, "didn't they?"

"They did. With better aim, too." Derek rubbed a head bump—perhaps imaginary, it was hard to see into his thick wiry hair.

"In the morning, the floor was slippery with monkey pee," Sue said to Richard. "It'd soaked right through the roof where they'd knocked off tiles."

"Now they seem to be gone—for the time being." Derek resumed eating.

"And then the centipedes came," Lila said, sitting up straight again.

Sue laughed. "Let's not scare Richard away on his first night back."

"You said we didn't have to be careful what we said around him anymore," Lila protested. Then she shut her mouth tight around a silent "oops."

No one else spoke either. Lila heard the cicadas grating away outside the house. Sweat trickled down her forehead. She looked round the table at her mother, her father, and at Richard. He gave her an off-kilter smile, one blue eye crinkling more than the other.

"You see, he's not upset." She pointed at his face.

"Oh, Lila." Sue sighed, then turned to Richard. "Well, how've things really been with you? You sounded so much better in your letters."

He let out a long breath. "I am," he said finally. "It started here."

"I thought so." Sue rested her fingers on his arm. "The workers still talk about the way you were with the buffaloes."

Lila remembered, too—how Richard had learned to wash them in the streams with long slow strokes of his hands along their flanks. His touch was so gentle that even the most restless beasts would turn their great heads and gaze contentedly at him as he hummed to them.

"He didn't know what buffaloes were till he came here," Lila said. "Until we showed him."

"We rescued him," Derek said to Sue suddenly, his eyes narrowing. "Now he's come back to rescue us."

Richard clunked down a forkful of cake. Crumbs scattered onto the table. "I never said anything like that."

"Of course he didn't." Sue glanced at Derek, then back at Richard. "Take another mango."

Lila's heart was thumping, the way it always did when her father said strange things. She pushed the mango bowl closer to Richard, then took one of the golden fruits out and placed it in his palm. "You just have to peel it, remember?" she asked in a quiet voice.

"I remember everything," Richard said. Then he turned to Derek. "You were good to me. So please—don't give me any shit now, okay?"

Derek stared back at him. His eyes were red-rimmed and slanted down at the corners, the way he looked when he'd taken medicine for his headaches. He wiped his lips with his napkin; when he put it down, the smile was back in his beard. "Only joking," he said. "Not to worry."

"All right." Richard started to peel the mango carefully with his knife. "Anyway...in the States, when things got tense, I always thought of this place, how bright and green it was. I *came back* here."

"In your mind?" Lila asked.

"Yeah. And I cheered up." Richard nodded. "I never did any more time, either."

"What—time?" Lila cocked her head.

"That means going to jail," Richard said, "which is where they used to put me after I'd done something stupid."

"Oh," Lila nodded. "I'm glad you didn't have to go there anymore."

She'd seen a kind of jail a few weeks ago when her "bus"—the little bullock cart that took her to school—

paused at the crossroads market behind a huge gray army van with wire mesh covering all the windows. Inside, people were packed in so close, standing up, that their faces were squashed against each others' shoulders and heads. They were Tamil terrorists on their way to a prison camp, her driver said. But the ones whose faces she could see through the mesh just looked like teenagers, not much older than her. A few were even girls. One girl had a long red gash across her face. A lot of the boys' eyes were puffed shut, and some had foreheads the horrible purple-yellow color of squashed fruit. Lila heard some of the terrorists sobbing, and in the middle of the vehicle, a boy shrieked like a pig being jabbed with a machete. After school, when Lila climbed onto the cart to go home, the prison van was still in the same place, still packed with people, but dreadfully silent. It had been baking in the sun all day, and now it radiated a stench like an overflowing latrine. For months afterwards, unable to forget it, Lila painted the van many times; each one grew taller and broader, a wheeled juggernaut among the tiny market stalls. Jagged red screams and brown stink-clouds shot out of the windows like flames. She was glad Richard hadn't seen one of those pictures in her portfolio, even though he did seem better.

He'd taken lots of jobs, he said, but for the last year he'd been working in a tree nursery in Colorado, and when he got back he was going to buy into the business with a woman who also worked there. They were probably going to get married. He passed around a photo of her. "Her name's Raquel," he told Lila. Raquel was dressed in clothes made of beaded cloth and yellow feathers, and seemed to be dancing, her arms raised and her black braids flying.

"American girls don't dress like that, do they?" Lila asked. She'd seen two American films in Colombo and knew that girls in the United States wore mini skirts and tight sweaters or black leather pants outfits.

"No, that's a dance costume." Richard smiled. "It's for a kind of religious festival called a powwow."

"Powwow," Lila repeated the words, her lips forming a smile around the sounds. "She's beautiful," she admitted. Raquel's skin was as dark as Lila's, with the same almond-shaped eyes as hers, only brown. Richard said her ancestors were mostly American Indian, with a little African and Spanish.

"Another hybrid. The loveliest roses are hybrids," Derek said, and smiled at Lila. He himself had a British grandmother, he'd once told her; even Sue was a hybrid, with ancestors from Ireland and Italy. Lila stared at the photo again; the feathers on the girl's arms ruffled, as if blown by wind.

The lamps were flickering. The fan blades jerked around slowly overhead as if trying to keep the electric current alive. The Buddha's-birthday-streamers swayed slowly. Then, as often happened, the power went off and the room seemed to fall into a black pit. Lila groaned, then cheered when Derek lit the paraffin lantern that was always on the dinner table.

One of her paintings showed her and Richard playing cards in a tent made of orange light. Now she fetched her own lantern from her bedroom, lit the wick, and stood on the couch to hang it from a long wire hook attached to a rafter. She took Richard's hand and pulled him into the tent with her.

"Cut!" she said, pointing to the deck of cards on the little table between them.

Richard sat down, then looked up at Derek, who was setting lit lanterns "for show" in all the front room's windows. "Want some help?" Richard asked him.

"No need, thanks. Daya's come." Derek pointed outside to where a flashlight beam was making long swipes through the foggy darkness. Then Derek was gone with his own flashlight, and through the window Lila could see the two figures on their way down the driveway, their beams sweeping through the tree branches.

"Papa checks the electrical wires to see if anybody's cut them," Lila said to Richard.

"The power's gone off a lot lately." Sue joined them at the little table.

"*Is* anyone cutting the wires?" Richard asked.

"No, no." Sue smiled. "Probably there's trouble at the power plant in Colombo. That's what the radio says."

"The government station?" Richard asked.

"It's still the only one we get." Sue glanced at the square radio on a little table in the kitchen hall.

Lila had the thought: with her father gone, Zalie might come back. She listened hopefully for the familiar mewing sound outside the nearest window. Then she was ashamed, picturing her father as he walked through the black fog, pushing away brambly underbrush.

"So you don't think anybody's really out there," Richard said to Sue.

"Well, there's some desperate souls roaming the roads these days," Sue said. "We're a little operation, making just enough to live on, but to those people we must look like a giant supermarket. You really can't blame poachers for wanting to get in."

"Are they Tamil refugees?" Richard asked.

"Some, probably. And some look like government soldiers who've thrown away their uniforms." Sue came over to the couch and spoke softly, as if she didn't want to be overheard. "The government—" she gestured toward the radio, "—never tells us everything that's going on."

During Richard's last visit, the terrorists were supposed to have been defeated. The radio had talked about victories and mopping-up operations (Lila drew soldiers swabbing out people's houses with huge, sudsy string-mops). But the fighting wasn't over at all, and now people said the government's army was retreating. All you heard on the radio, though, were cricket scores, film music, and security bulletins. One bulletin said that it was against the law to talk about the war, and evidently, Lila learned, this meant even to your friends at school recess. The head teacher had lectured the students about this. You could be arrested for starting rumors or saying anything bad about the government—though Derek sometimes said (in a hushed voice at supper) that a lot of politicians were thieves.

"Doesn't Derek have a short-wave?" Richard asked.

"He said he was going to buy one last time he went to Colombo...." Sue's voice faded.

"But you do have cell phones now, don't you?"

"We've got four," Lila said. "Mine's blue!" She jumped down from the couch and ran barefoot into her dark room. By touch, she found the cool plastic phone on her bedside table, and took it to Richard. "It's like a walkie-talkie, too. I can talk to Papa outside—" She climbed onto the couch, leaning against Richard, and tapped the buttons with her fingertips.

"Nothing's lighting up," Sue said. "You haven't charged it, dear."

"I forgot." She glanced at the shelf beside the front door. There, hanging from a wire from a light fixture, was the battery charger; a green phone was plugged into it. "Papa's phone's here. He forgot to take it with him!"

"We've only just got these things," Sue told Richard. "It's hard to remember to keep them going."

"Sorry," Lila said. The exclamation marks, she noticed, were digging into Richard's forehead again. She felt her own forehead to see if she had any. It was hard to tell.

"I wish Derek weren't out there in the dark," Richard said. "But then we're all in the dark, aren't we?"

"The electricity always comes on eventually," Sue said.

Lila stared at the lantern's glare reflecting on the black window panes, and for the first time she didn't want to think what might be outside. But wait—Zalie was outside, she told herself. And her father was. "We've got lots of lanterns," she told Richard. "And plenty of paraffin."

Richard pressed his lips together, squinting as if he were trying hard to figure something out. "I'm still a little jumpy, I guess...."

"It's probably just the *gevala preta* spirits," Lila said, and felt calmer. "They have to get used to you being here again."

"That's all we need," Sue said. "Thank you, Miss."

"What did she say?" Richard smiled again. "Am I being watched by invisible beings?"

"The local people fill her head with all sorts of ghost stories, and she paints gruesome pictures of them." Sue rolled her eyes.

"They're not all gruesome." Still, Lila thought, it might be a good idea if she waited until daylight to show the pictures to Richard. "I'll deal," she said, picking up the cards and flipping them out, snap-snap-snap the way he'd taught her.

Richard picked up his cards, but didn't look at them right away. He seemed to be listening for something.

THREE

The next morning Lila rose before dawn to bathe with the local women in the spring-pool so she could listen to their gossip and stories. Then she climbed a lime tree to wait for Richard to get up, and also to look for her cat, which was still missing. The clouds opened like silver pods as long gaps of red sunlight burnt through them. The tall palms caught the light first, their jagged heads silhouetted along the hillsides; in Lila's pictures, they were shaggy demon-dancers waving torches over the valley. Past the house, on the other side of the road, the light flowed into the water-filled paddy fields, turning them to mirrors reflecting the sky. White cranes glided over the water's surface, wings flapping slowly. All around her, birds squawked and shrieked, amazed by the light as if they'd never seen it before today.

Lila picked some limes and swung down into the tall grass. Then she took a path to the hut of the rubber tapper who took care of one of her family's buffaloes. No one there had seen Zalie. The tapper's wife gave Lila a pail of milk, which Lila took to the house, pausing to take sips.

"Mum, has Zalie come back?" she shouted as she pushed open the screened back door. Strangely, the cat's two bowls were missing from their spot in the corner of the kitchen.

Sue, who was on a different level of consciousness, didn't answer. She was seated in a lotus position on a mat in the little prayer alcove near the laundry room, the backs of her hands resting on her knees, her fingers curled upward as if balancing bubbles. Her eyelids were nearly closed, like those of the small stone Buddha facing her from its altar.

Lila had helped make the altar from a wooden tea-chest and swathes of red velvet. The incense smoking in the brass tray beside the image smelled of cinnamon. Lila's own meditation today had lasted only a minute; *The jewel is in the blossom of the lotus,* she'd whispered a dozen times, and gave up. Still agitated by Richard's presence in the house, she couldn't keep thoughts and pictures from jumping around in her brain like frogs.

She found Richard's room empty; since he'd said last night he wanted to bathe in the spring (the men had their turn after the women every morning), that must be where he was. Derek was out on his rounds checking fences. She lay down on the couch in the sitting room to wait. She seemed always to be waiting these days—for Richard, of course, ever since his last letters, but also for...she didn't know what. She scratched an itchy bug-bite, and wiped the sweat from her forehead with her sleeve. The morning heat gave the flowers outside the windows a strong fermented scent that she'd never noticed before. Though the fan was off, faint currents were moving through the air as if somebody were walking around the room. It wasn't one of the childlike *preta* spirits who dashed around like little breezes, but someone slower, more elderly and ponderous. Lila had a feeling that the house's former owner was back, grumbling to himself about the way her father wasn't taking proper care of the property, and wondering what Richard was doing here. Lila didn't know why Richard had come, either, but she wouldn't ask; she might sound as if she expected him to do something that he would finish and then go away again—back to Raquel in her beautiful feathered dress and braids. A real red Indian! Who wouldn't want to go back to someone like that? Lila sighed.

Now she heard her mother leaving the meditation area and padding into the kitchen to start making breakfast. Water gushed into a kettle. The fridge opened and clicked shut. The ponderous presence slunk away.

Lila tiptoed into Richard's room, where a translucent mosquito net had been draped over a rectangular frame above the bed. On the bedside table lay a thin, shiny plastic box. Lila couldn't stop herself from picking it up. It was smooth like the cell phones but black, elegant, heavy. She discovered a panel that slid sideways to reveal a long dial. It was a new radio, with a chrome aerial on top that she pulled out and out until it was as long as her arm. But she could make it play only frantic squeals. She quickly switched it off and put it back on the table. Then she heard a voice—Richard's; he was in the kitchen with Mum. She ran out of his room.

"…living in a dream world!" he finished a sentence as Lila stopped outside the doorway.

"Derek's been so busy getting the nature sanctuary ready," Sue said. "I wrote you—"

"Hello," Lila said. She pushed aside the bead curtains that hung from the top of the door frame, entering the room with a flourish-like clicking sound. "What did you write, Mum?"

Sue lifted the steaming kettle from the stove. She looked older this morning, her high cheeks tight, her lips drawn. Lila noticed a few strands of gray in her red-brown curls. She wore a long cotton shirt over a pair of faded jeans. "Just a letter," she said. "Did you sleep well?"

"I've been up for *hours.*" Lila looked from her mother to Richard. His wet hair was combed back from his forehead. "Why did you stop talking when I came in?" she asked her mother. "You never do that." She was never left out of adult conversations; sometimes she even lay at the foot of her parents' bed to listen to them talk until she fell asleep.

"Because you surprised us, silly!" Sue brushed some twigs out of Lila's hair. Lila squirmed; this wasn't a real answer.

Richard squatted down beside her. "I need you to show me around again after breakfast."

"Sure. I'll show you everything."

Lila cut up limes for her and Richard's curd. In America, he said, curd was called "yogurt"; it came in plastic containers and was full of sweet chemicals. Lila asked why he didn't get a buffalo. He explained that people didn't have them in America. Lila shook her head, her blue eyes wide. Almost everything at the table had been grown on the plantation, Sue told Richard, who seemed to find this as extraordinary as Lila did the absence of domestic buffaloes in the United States. Millet porridge, mangoes, pineapple, pawpaw, bananas, rice cakes, vegetables, cassava-flour bread, rambutan jelly, no meat, of course, and tea…well, the tea was from Derek's uncle's place in the highlands; it didn't grow well this far south. Derek wasn't speaking to this uncle nowadays, nor to one of his brothers. They were planning to flee the country; Derek and an aunt in Colombo were suing to keep them from taking family money with them. Sue thought it was a shame that Derek was cutting himself off from his family. Lila, who'd heard all this before, drummed her fingers against the table until Richard finally finished eating.

Then she took him to see the vegetable garden, which he'd helped to double in size two years ago. It still produced plenty of cabbages, chilies, beans, lentils, potatoes, and cauliflowers, though leafy vines had grown over it so you couldn't tell which was garden and which was wild vegetation until you felt around under the leaves. She and Richard went to look at the rubber trees that grew on the hill that sloped down to the paddy fields. Along the coast road, Richard said, he'd seen rubber trees growing in neat rows with grass between them; small stainless steel pails were clipped to the bottom of the spirals cut into each tree's trunk. But here the trees grew unevenly, with scrub bushes scattered among them and coconut half-shells tied to the trunks with old twine to collect the white sap. Fruit grew everywhere among other vegetation, but unless you remembered exactly where it was, you might lose half your crop.

"We all remember where everything is, though," Lila said.

He nodded. "This place is so fertile, you could live for quite a while just on things that fall out of the trees."

"Mum says it's paradise here," Lila said.

"I know she does. I can see why." Richard walked slowly as if he wanted to absorb as much green-tinted light as possible. "You know, she and I grew up on a farm where nothing grew but rocks," he said. "In winter, the earth was frozen muck and the sky turned to gray ice. After I finally got out of there, it took me years to stop shivering."

"Mum doesn't like to talk about that place."

Richard nodded. "The town—well, you had to raise a lot of hell to keep from suffocating. It was your mom and me against the world. But she got away to college, that's what saved her."

"She said Papa saved her. And Buddha."

"Them, too, sure," Richard said. "Anyway, when I first came here, I looked up at that hot blue sky and smelled those white flowers in the bushes—" He mopped his forehead with his sleeve. "I thought I was in Heaven, too."

"That's good," Lila said. "But were you still cold?"

"Yeah. The old weather and nastiness kept echoing inside me. And then, when I arrived and you said, 'Hello, Uncle Richard,' in that warm little British voice of yours—"

"It's not British."

"It is, some. You must have picked up the accent at school or from your father. It's pretty, sort of lilting." He made a soaring movement in the air with his hand." Your voice started to de-frost me. It's hard to explain, but I just wanted you to keep talking to me."

Lila squinted up at him. No one had ever spoken to her like this before. She didn't know what to say so she just took his hand, and they walked on down the path. All the trees and plants looked different today; she pictured them gazing at Richard from eyes on their leaves, waiting to see what he'd do. The buzz of cicadas made a hovering cloud around her, and in the trees a gecko lizard chuckled metallically. Something moved among the bushes behind a gap in the bamboo fence.

"Zalie?" Lila called out, but it wasn't the cat, it was something much bigger. She heard a faint, fast galloping of hooves. The bushes' leaves seemed to gasp as the animal sped past them. She stared hard into the jungle but saw only a ripple in the wall of green. It vanished as the sound quickly faded. "Did you hear that?" Lila said, pressing her hand to her heart. Her whole chest thumped.

"Yeah!" Richard was still squinting into the underbrush. "A wild deer, right?"

"A *sambhur!*" Lila spoke in a hushed voice. "You hardly ever see them, you just hear them out there."

Richard smiled. "Maybe we'll get lucky and see one someday."

"Maybe."

Now the path gave onto an old clay roadway that once had been wide enough for a car or bullock cart. To her left, it led to a stone house drooping vines from a corrugated metal roof. Tenants used to live there; now it was empty, Lila said—at least her father thought so.

"It doesn't look empty to me," Richard said.

He was right. Purplish smoke was rising through the trees near the house, and a bare patch of earth had been cleared beside it.

"Papa says not to go near it, just in case."

"Okay."

They turned right. The roadway led along the partially collapsed bamboo fence to an old gate made of heavy planks. They had recently been crisscrossed with new barbed wire that shone like silver twine in the sunlight. The whole plantation was fenced in, more or less, by bamboo and wire. On the other side of this gate was the public road.

Lila stopped, squeezing Richard's hand. A group of barefoot boys about her age were standing around outside the fence in dirty shorts. When they spotted Lila and Richard, they took several steps backward, snickering.

"What do you want?" Lila demanded in Sinhala.

"Fuck off, half-breed!" the biggest boy said in the same language.

"You fuck off!" Lila rammed her hands on her hips. "You're always trying to steal fruit. I know you!"

"You don't know what goes on around here." The boy laughed, his nose wrinkling. "Your father's crazy as the German!"

"He's stingy!" another boy said.

"He's not!" Lila shouted.

The boys laughed. Some of them were glancing up into the tree over Lila's head, but she just wiped her nose with her wrist and glared straight at them.

Richard stepped between her and the boys. "Let's go," he said to her. "Look—" He gestured toward a boy in a ragged shirt who was sitting on the ground next to the nearest fence post.

At first Lila didn't notice much about him but the pinkish ringworm patches in his black hair. Then she saw something in his hand that looked like a long knife with a metal handle. He poked the post with the point, making a rhythmic thunking noise that throbbed in the air. On and on it went, like a big beak pecking—methodical, mindless, violent. The chipping away at the heavy wood had no effect on the fence, but the boy kept at it, sweat dripping down his face.

"That's a bayonet!" Richard said. "Where the hell did he get that?"

"They find them or steal them." Lila kept her voice calm, but she edged closer to Richard. "They carry military stuff around to look tough. One boy had a grenade last week."

"Christ." Richard squinted at the boys.

The strange thing was, nobody but Richard and Lila seemed to hear the thunking sound. The boys were all looking up into the tree. Suddenly Richard jumped back, yanking Lila with him. Thump! Something landed on the ground right in front of her—a small boy had just fallen out of the branches. A whoop went up. Now the boy was scrambling along the ground on all fours. He dove headfirst under the gate, his hands scrabbling ahead of him in the dirt.

Several of his friends rushed to pull him out. Around his shoulder was a burlap sack spilling rambutan fruits. The gate's wire left long red scratches in the bare flesh of his back.

Staggering to his feet, he raced off with the others, his face clenched in grinning rage. Everything happened so quickly that all Lila or Richard could do was stare at the boys as they scrambled down the slope on the other side of the road. Then they reappeared farther away, racing off between the paddy fields.

Richard let go of Lila's hand to wipe his face. Some ordinary green parrots flew over, and the back-to-normal insect sounds of the plantation started up again. Were things back to normal? Or had something changed? Lila squeezed her fists at her sides.

"I'm sorry those boys were so rude," she said.

"I wish I could have done something." Richard kicked a rock into the brush. "I didn't even know what they were saying to you. What was it?"

"Nothing much," she said. "They don't like Papa."

"The land-owner."

"Boys are always stealing fruit."

Richard narrowed his eyes. "It's been a while since I saw people running like that—not for a race or for fun, but to really escape and survive."

"Who did you see like that before?"

"Well, me, among others."

Lila gazed up at him. When he moved his face a little sideways, trying to smile, she noticed for the first time that one of his side teeth was missing. "Come on," she said, "I'll show you the sanctuary."

The entire plantation eventually would be a nature park, her father had told her. Beds of flowers, clusters of huge green plants, small trees festooned with luxuriant red bell-shaped flowers or hung with blue-blossoming vines—all were bordered by wire security fences. Richard walked with his shoulders hunched. Lila could see that he was upset by all the fences, but she busied herself opening gates in front of her and closing them behind her as she walked along; she was in charge of the paths. She often came here carrying Zalie, playing the tour guide. "That's going to be the place for families to sit," she said to Richard, pointing to an open area where low cement cylinders were positioned upright in the grass. "Wood table tops are going to rest on them, and there'll be umbrellas and folding chairs." Richard nodded, staring at the cylinders. They were stained with the vertical drip marks that rains leave on cement structures in the tropics, making them look old and shabby after only a few seasons. "There's going to be a snacks kiosk, and a fridge for cold drinks," Lila announced.

Richard picked up a sign from the grass. The wood was crumbling along the edges and the words *REST AREA* were almost too faded to read. "I helped Derek paint this sign—only two years ago," he said, and his voice trailed off.

Lila scratched her head, staring at it. When her father described the sanctuary to her, she could picture parties of school children having tea and biscuits at the tables and running along the paths. But now she saw more clearly than before the knee-high grass and the stained cement stumps and the wild, snarled vegetation shoving its way into the gardens from all sides.

"Do you want to see the zoo?" Lila ran past Richard. "We're going to have an elephant!"

He set the sign down in the grass. "Why an elephant?"

"I don't know," she said in a suddenly small voice. Some girls at school had asked her the same question, so after a while she stopped talking about her father's sanctuary to them. You can see elephants on the roads dragging logs any time, they said in their nasal mocking voices; they walk around the park in Colombo. Nobody'll ever come all the way out here to see a silly elephant! The girls didn't understand how long her father had been talking about the sanctuary—how many bushes and flowers and trees he and the workers had planted, how many nights he'd sat up drawing maps and blueprints, writing letters to government ministries, reading books on wildlife management. It wasn't too hard to ignore the question "Why an elephant?" when those stupid girls asked it. They liked to rag her for looking different, anyway, and for constantly drawing pictures of things that nobody else cared about or even noticed. But she couldn't ignore Richard. She ran back to him.

"Come on!" she cried, but he still didn't move. So she grabbed his hand and dug her heels into the ground to tug.

"Whoa!" He sprawled onto the long grass, and she fell beside him.

Laughing, she crawled up onto his back and sat cross-legged. "Why did you stop?" she asked, out of breath.

"I was attacked by a giant python," he groaned.

"No, you weren't!" she laughed. "Why did you stop?"

"I'll tell you if you get the python off me."

She slid down and leaned her elbow against his shoulder, waiting.

"The truth is, Lila—" He turned toward her. "I don't much like seeing creatures in cages."

"Really it's for their own good," she said. "Poachers are always coming in after *sambhurs* and other animals for food.

They even steal monkeys to sell in Europe."

"So the animals will be in protective custody here," Richard said.

She wasn't sure what he meant; his face was clouded over and she didn't want to ask. "And there's other creatures we've been feeding for years," she went on. "Baby bush pigs, birds that are almost extinct. Mum leaves food out for them." Lila jumped up, brushing grass off her skirt. "Some of them only know how to live in captivity, not on the outside."

"I heard about that." Richard got to his feet and looked up the path to the zoo area, his eyes narrowing. Ahead was a long cement structure that rose about a foot above the shaggy grass. It contained seven rectangular sunken areas that looked like the floors of cages, but except for two chicken-wire pens at one end, there were no enclosures yet, just waiting air.

"The only actual animal Papa's got so far is a tortoise," Lila said. "After we look at it, we'll go if you want. It's getting hot, anyway."

"Right." Richard walked beside her again.

The tortoise was about ten inches long, with a spiky gold and black pattern on his shell—just the sort of thing the locals would steal, Derek had said. They'd make soup out of him and then sell his shell for a thousand rupees to some tourist at a coast hotel. Now he lay on a flat stone in a cage that was about four feet square and as high as Lila's waist. The tortoise's ancient head was motionless, his hooded eyes closed.

"He's beautiful," Richard said.

"Papa says he'll outlive all of us." Lila poked her finger through the cage.

Richard smiled, squatting down. "What's his name?"

"Thomas," Lila said. "Though I don't know if he really needs a name. He just sits there."

"Everybody needs a name," Richard said.

"In the mornings, we bring him fresh water and greens."

"I'm sure he's glad to see you, in his way," Richard said. Then he pointed to the other cage, a wire enclosure about twice the size of the tortoise's. "What's in this one?" he asked.

Lila hadn't looked into it. "Nothing," she said, kneeling down to poke a leaf in front of Thomas's beaky mouth.

"I thought I heard something move."

"That cage's been open forever," Lila said, wiping her forehead. The insects were buzzing around her now, and she wanted to get back to the cool of the house.

"But its door's been shut tight."

"Oh." Now Lila looked. "You're right."

"It's locked." Richard pointed to a fresh-cut wooden peg stuck in the wire latch of the cage's metal gate.

"I never saw that peg before." Lila leaned sideways. The sun's heat seemed to soak through her back to her stomach, making her feel queasy. Now she wanted to run back to the house. Off balance, she leaned against Richard to squint into the shade at the far end of the cage: a miniature jungle of leafy weeds and long coarse grass.

The grass twitched. She heard a faint, high-pitched mewing.

FOUR

Lila ran back from the zoo ahead of Richard and ploughed face-first into her mother, knocking her off balance. Sue had just stood up from planting flowers along the driveway; now the trowel slipped from her fingers as she heard Lila's report on what she'd seen at the zoo. "Zalie's in jail! Just because of that squirrel!" Lila finished, her voice ragged.

"I'm so sorry, dear." Sue took a long breath.

"It's not fair!" Lila bit her lip.

"I know." Susan shook her head. "But I'm sure your father's got some kind of reason."

Richard came down the path toward her. "What reason?" he asked. His forehead furrowed into two vertical lines. "For Chrissake, it's the nature of cats to hunt—"

Sue clutched his arm. "Please, Rich, don't get into this."

"I wanted to unlock the cage door," he said. "But Lila said that'd cause more trouble."

"It would have." Sue sighed. "But things will be all right. I'll ask Derek about it right away."

"Will you?" Richard asked.

"I said I will! Damn it, you don't understand how things are around here!"

Richard pried her fingers off his arm but held onto them gently. "Do *you* understand? Does *he?*"

"I don't know!" Sue cleared her throat, then turned back to Lila. "We'll have Zalie out in a day or two, I'm positive."

"Okay." Lila sniffled.

Why did her father do such strange things? She almost hated him now. But that felt like a strange thing to do, too. She walked away, scuffing her sandals hard against the grass. Ahead of her, the afternoon light swam golden and green among the trees, like sunbeams waving in water, but smudges of dark gray smoke were rising from the rubber-treatment shed, and the acrid smell of heated sap was sticky in the air. Bare-chested men in sarongs were shoveling coconut husks through a wide doorway through which Lila could see women setting them out on the glowing coals. Other men were hanging mats of black rubber over beams to cool. Everyone was smudged black, the whites of their eyes glowing out of the shadows. When Derek stepped into the light, his blue slacks and bush shirt were drenched with sweat; he wiped his face with a handkerchief. Lila could see that his eyes were damp and squinted, and she knew that one of his excruciating headaches was coming over him.

Returning to the house, she and her father sat side by side on a sofa in the living room; Sue and Richard stood at a distance. "It must be hard to accept at first, I know," Derek told Lila in his quiet voice. Had he heard her protests through the walls of the shed? He must have. "So let's think. It's true that Zalie shouldn't have been let out to do just anything she wanted to do, isn't it?" He rested his hand on Lila's shoulder so softly that tears came to her eyes, and she nodded slowly.

"I'm the one who didn't watch Zalie." She wiped her cheek. "Shouldn't I be punished, instead?"

"We have no pen that would fit you!" He tried to make his voice light. Then he sighed. "In a way, you are being punished. It doesn't seem fair, I know, but it's necessary. And perhaps it can help everyone here to learn about valuing life—the way Zalie did not."

"How can it?" Sue's eyes burned behind her glasses.

"People will be reminded that we cannot tolerate bloodshed getting into our sanctuary," Derek said. "It's especially important nowadays with so much trouble in the

North. That's far away, I know. But the atmosphere of violence is floating down here, and people here are breathing it in. They're hardly aware of what it's doing to them."

Lila nodded, remembering the boys at the gate.

"But here we're an example of peace. We've got discipline and harmony." Derek wiped his eyes. "Keeping our harmony with each other, with nature—this is the best way we can stay safe."

Sue sat down on the couch opposite. "I think there are other ways, Derek."

"Oh, yes. And I'm working on them as well, don't worry." Derek glanced at her and Richard, then back at Lila. "Anyway, this harmony can flow out of here into the countryside...." He moved his fingers gracefully through the air, and Lila could picture currents of kindness blowing down the driveway and gliding like white cranes across the paddy fields.

"I pray for harmony," Sue whispered.

"And meanwhile," Derek said. "Old Zalie gets to lie about in her own tropical rest home for a few days, all shady and cool. Safe from poachers, too."

Sue's eyes blinked open. "Oh, Derek, who's going to steal a cat?"

"It's not as if people ate them," Richard said. He leaned awkwardly against the side of the couch as if he didn't quite know where to position himself in the room. "Do they?"

Derek turned slowly to him. "Our people have never eaten cats in all our many centuries of dominating this island. While Portuguese sailors were chewing on mice to survive their passages here, and while the American settlers were eating each other on the Western trails—"

Sue frowned. "Derek, please—get off it!"

"The Donner party, the Mormon handcart expeditions—they were in our history books at university, Sue—remember?" He smiled at her, then glared at Richard. "At any rate, during all these noble times of European expansion, the Sinhalese rulers of Ceylon stayed home and lived lives of refinement. Constantly they were making sure their subjects were well fed—no felines, no rodents, no *homo sapiens* in anyone's diets."

Lila gazed at her father. "Did people really eat other people in America?"

"Very occasionally."

"I never would!" Lila squeaked. "Anyway, we're vegetarians!"

"But the original question—why would anyone harm Zalie?" Derek's eyes were thoughtful and warm. "Consider this, my darling. Think about the boys who hang about the gates. Always trying to sneak in to steal fruit, deer, boars. What are they like?"

"Mean," Lila said.

"Yes. And wouldn't they like to take out their frustrations on our pet, if they found it strolling on the road?"

Sue shifted her position behind the sofa. "I suppose you're right."

Derek gently squeezed Lila's shoulder. "Do you see the point, too, Miss?"

Lila was about to say she did. Then she glanced up at Richard, whose forehead was still lined, and she couldn't say anything.

"I'm still having trouble following everything you've said," Richard said to Derek.

Derek nodded. "It must be hard for you to understand this country of ours." The word "ours," Lila thought, was intended to include everyone but Richard. But now she felt that she, too, was becoming un-included from somewhere she'd never questioned her place in before.

While her parents talked, Lila distracted herself by doing a sketch of her friend Radha Sharma, who complained that her parents left her out of things, too. Her father was a doctor and her mother a nurse at the crossroads clinic. Though they were Tamil Hindus, they kept photos of Buddhist temples on their waiting room walls, along with pictures of pop-eyed devil dancer masks. There was a drawing of the Moslems' holy building, the Kaba'a, which looked like a beautiful big slab of black rock. Beside it was a framed print of the baby Jesus and his mother, Mary. Mary looked a lot like the Hindu goddess Laxmi in the print on the opposite wall, though Mary's bosom wasn't nearly as round as Laxmi's. (Lila often noticed bosoms these days because she was waiting impatiently for her own to pop up on her chest. Plump Radha, who was nearly thirteen, already had breasts that filled the bodice of her new saris.) The point of all the pictures, Radha's parents said, was to help people of all faiths—even animists—to feel comfortable about coming to the clinic and using Western medicine.

The harmony didn't extend far beyond pictures on the walls, though. Lila and Radha, reading or sketching on the carpet in the house's living room, frequently heard Radha's parents shouting down the hallways. Her mother insisted that it wasn't safe any longer for them to stay here. Her family in Canada would help them if they emigrated. Radha's father, whose horn-rimmed glasses magnified the weary bags under his eyes, pointed out that most of his patients were poor Sinhalese peasants who had trusted him for years and would never harm his family. How could she think of deserting them now when they needed the clinic more than ever? Radha's mother gasped, "I know, I know, but..." and then burst into tears. The fight resumed behind the closed door of the bedroom.

Lila's parents' bedroom door was never closed. They never shouted or wept; Lila would have heard them. Lila looked up from her sketch. "D'you think a bad *preta* spirit's got into Zalie?" she asked suddenly. "Some of the women once told me..." Her voice trailed off.

Richard gave her a quizzical look.

Sue suddenly stood up. "Is that it, Derek?"

"I don't know," he said. "We'll just have to wait and see what happens."

"But why Zalie?" Lila pushed her feet hard into the floor.

"I'm not an expert in these things. But if I have to consult experts, I promise I will." Derek squeezed the bridge of his nose, his eyes nearly shut. That meant he had to take headache medicine. Standing up, he blinked away tears, and went into the bedroom. A minute later he was rushing out the front door again to continue his patrol of the fences and walk off his pain. Lila stood in the doorway, watching him move down the drive.

*

Lila visited Zalie, bringing her things to eat and drink. And of course the cat was perfectly all right, as Sue said it would be; Zalie spent most of her time sleeping and eating, anyway. Now Lila never had to worry where she'd wandered off to, she told herself. She and Richard had nailed some planks together to make a sloping roof over the cage to keep the sun and rain off both the cat and the tortoise in the next cage. Sue let Lila put down blankets next to Zalie's cage so that she could stay there and keep her company in the shade of a grapefruit tree.

As she lay on the blankets, Lila sketched "cartoons," which was what Leonardo da Vinci did in her mother's Art History book. Then she used them to paint a larger picture with pastels: an enormous prison van that towered over not only crossroads market stalls but the school and clinic, too. An animal that looked something like Zalie and something like the lion on the Sri Lanka flag broke down one wall of the van, turning the window-grates to tangles of wire with one paw-swipe. Soldiers fled like squirrels with bushy tails. Then the cat-lion acquired orange tigerish stripes. Suddenly Lila realized that someone (her head teacher, for instance) might think that the cat was a Tiger with a capital T, and have her arrested for drawing subversive propaganda. So she filled in the stripes with more orange. It was smudged now. The beast looked as if it were melting. For a while she reread a book that Richard had once mailed her, *Navajo Tales: Ghosts and Warriors*. Then she began a new sketch: Raquel spread her yellow-feathered arms and soared over the plantation's palm trees. Beside her flew a smaller girl with a face the same shade of gold and green parrot wings....

Zalie began mewing again. It occurred to Lila what a strange situation this was—her bringing bowls of milk and food to the cat the way she brought greens to the tortoise. She wondered if the two elderly animals were friends. It was strange the way she thought about Zalie so often now. This made her change the way she thought about her father, and her mother, and even Richard.

When she spoke to Papa, she was careful to avoid saying something that might make him lengthen Zalie's "holiday." Yet Derek didn't like Lila speaking carefully to him; he would tickle her or make outrageous statements just to get spontaneous responses from her. When only sullen complaints resulted, he withdrew from her, making her feel she'd done something wrong. Then she wanted to scream at him. This had never happened before.

Her mother seemed strangely over-generous nowadays, putting extra sugar into her tea, spending the afternoon making *kulfi*—Indian ice cream—for her in the freezer trays. Lila said things to her—"I don't like cinnamon on my *kulfi!*"—which ordinarily would have gotten her a laugh or a light smack on the bottom but now merely elicited a sigh. Lila found herself thinking up meaner things to say to her mother and then feeling like an even worse brat.

The whole plantation had changed over the past few days. Clouds seemed to have shifted somewhere overhead. A strange light lingered over the countryside. Shadows lay along the ground like dark smudges. And she was sure she heard Zalie's faint mewing even when she was much too far away to hear any sound from the zoo cage. It was more like a sensation in the air than a sound, and at night, it made her restless while she played cards with Richard or tried to meditate with her mother. Later, lying in bed, she heard faint rustlings outside her window as if something were pacing back and forth there, brushing against leaves and grass, and sighing. She'd heard them before; often she'd been told that such sounds—or sensations, or whatever they were—were made by a *preta* who was upset about being abandoned between its last life and its next life. Now, in a way, she knew how it felt. The being seemed to know her. It wanted her to feel how sad and restless it was. As she drifted off to sleep, she felt as if she might be a *preta* herself, stuck between incarnations. She was aching for her old familiar life…but at the same time longing for everything to change….

But now it was afternoon, not night, and Lila was just waking from a doze beside Zalie's cage, her cheek resting on her sketch pad. She heard people's voices. Sitting up, she caught a glimpse of her mother's long cotton skirt swinging through the grass down the path. Richard was walking beside her in his wide-brimmed hat and jeans and denim jacket. Lila got to her feet and walked quietly behind them.

"I'm sort of in the same position you are with Derek," she heard Richard say.

"How is that?" Sue asked.

Richard chewed on a blade of grass. "Raquel's gradually taken up a whole belief system, too. Everything she sees either makes her feel in harmony with her people's ways, or it alienates her from them. If I disagree with her—like I tell her grinding up blue corn a certain way probably isn't going to cure her cousin's flu—then I'm suspect. I'm an outsider who doesn't know anything about the spirit world, or some damn thing—"

"It's not some damn thing." Sue walked more slowly, taking Richard's arm to step over a fallen log. Lila waited before jumping over it, staying out of her mother's line of vision.

"So you really believe in this stuff, too?" Richard asked.

"What, Buddhism? Of course I do." Sue turned to smile at him.

"No, I meant the demons and spells and so forth."

She sighed. "You're not surrounded by it day and night like I am. You haven't seen the strange things that go on here!" Sue held Richard's arm tighter. "I tried to dismiss it at first. Sometimes I wanted to shake Derek by the collar and scream in his face—wise up! This is voodoo! You've got a masters degree in biology!"

"Did you ever try it?"

"Several times. He laughed and agreed with me

completely. And then went off and did whatever he thought he needed to do."

"Like what?"

"Well, I know he consults various healers. I don't understand that much about them, but I know I can't afford to ignore the things that they believe in."

"Religious things," Richard said, looking carefully at her. "Listen, I'm just trying to understand."

"Yes, religious. And animist, and political, too. It's all mixed up together here, especially nowadays."

"I heard the BBC this morning." Richard tapped his fingers against something hard, and Lila saw that he was carrying his small black radio. "In Colombo, the politicians are debating about another troop withdrawal. But really the government's troops are being overrun."

"In the North," Sue said.

"Not all that far—"

"Politics here are a nightmare." Sue cut him off. "Anyway—Derek's taking native medicine again."

"Oh, shit!" Richard kicked a stone on the path.

"I suppose it's all right. I mean, it's the stuff all the villagers take. Nothing the doctor's given him at the clinic did any good." She stopped, staring up at Richard through her blurred spectacles. "I can't do a thing to help him, either, no matter how hard I try. That's the worst part for me. When the pain comes over him…" Sue pressed both her hands over her cheeks, then dropped them to her side. "It's bad for Lila, too."

Hearing her name, Lila walked a little more quickly, closing the distance between her and her mother.

"You know how she's always drawing pictures," Sue went on. "I don't like to make comments—it's her own world, and she needs it—but last week she did a pastel I had to ask her about. It looked like a man inside a glass bubble. The man had a beard...."

"Her father?"

"That's what I asked her. And when she said yes...well, I knew exactly what it meant."

Lila nearly tripped over a root. She felt like shouting before her mother could say anything more—already she felt her cheeks burning with a kind of scary embarrassment. But she also wanted badly to hear what Sue would say about the drawing.

"The air inside the glass was a dark smoky color. The figure in the bubble seemed to be dissolving in the smoke—the pain—but he couldn't get out," Sue said.

Richard nodded. "And nobody could get to him."

"That's right. He was cut off from everyone, alone."

Richard shook his head. "That's hard."

"In the picture, Lila understood all that."

"She must miss him."

Lila had to push her knuckles against her lips to keep from screaming, now. She stumbled on along the uneven ground.

"What did you say to her?" Richard asked.

Sue shook her head. "Nothing. I should have told her what I saw. I should have said *something*. But when I looked at the painting and I suddenly got it, I didn't want her to see my face. So I sort of hugged her against my chest...."

"I *saw* your face!" Lila shouted, and suddenly pitched forward. She grabbed for a tree branch to keep from falling, and swung with it. The path seemed to tilt sideways. "I *saw* you! You were crying!"

Sue and Richard both stopped, turned, and stared at her. Lila gripped the branch in both hands, almost hanging from it. She felt as if she'd been caught playing in some dangerous way; she also felt foolish, unable to let go of the branch, lest she flop onto her face.

"Lila!" Sue took a step toward her, arms out. "Where did you come from?"

"You've been tailing us, haven't you?" Richard reached her first. He picked her up by the waist in both hands; the branch flew out of her grip as he put her down on the path. She was so dizzy that she collapsed against her mother. She felt her mother's arm go around her; it was tight against her shoulder.

"Sorry," she squeaked. "I was...curious to hear."

Sue leaned over so that her hair brushed Lila's cheek. "What big ears you have, Lila!"

She covered them. "I haven't."

"Well, there's worse things." Sue's arm softened but still held her.

Richard ruffled Lila's hair. "You didn't hear anything you couldn't handle, right?" he asked, and she nodded, wiping her eyes on her mother's blouse. "We're all worried about your father."

"I heard Dr. Sharma say that Papa's got chronic pain something," Lila said.

"Chronic pain syndrome," Sue said. "That's the Western way of describing it."

"Western?" Lila asked, staring up at her mother's face.

"A doctor's way," Sue said.

Richard cocked his head to one side, staring at Sue, and Lila could see her mother give him a look back.

"Don't you start on me again, Richie," she said. "I'll smack you, I swear I will! Like I did when we were little."

He laughed. "Your mother was a holy terror when she was your age," he said to Lila.

"She was?" Lila grinned.

"Now she's just holy."

Sue reached over Lila's head and cuffed Richard behind the ear. "Don't say I didn't warn you." Richard's hat went whirling off into the underbrush.

Lila let out a whoop and dashed after it.

FIVE

Lila suspected that her mother had talked to her father about the picture of the man in the glass bubble, because Derek started taking her on his rounds again, showing her the burrows of tiny animals and new species of plants to sketch as they checked fences and gates. Some of the men passing in the road hurried by without greeting Derek. He explained that they were probably angry that he wouldn't let them in to take wild fruit or to hunt; they had little idea about nature preservation yet, but the sanctuary's educational programs would help them understand their natural heritage better.

Once or twice a week, Lila went with her mother on visits to workers' wives around the plantation. She helped give out bandages and aspirins, read and wrote letters for people, admired new babies, sat on steps to shell peas with her mother and the Sinhalese or Tamil women as they all chatted. Lila had been coming on these visits since she'd been small enough to ride on her mother's shoulders; she loved tramping along the old paths that wound through the plantation.

She and her mother lifted fallen boughs out of their way and stopped by streams to wash the sweat from their faces. Lila ran ahead to part leafy branches; they were curtains that opened out on clearings where children played games and people piled coconuts and chopped wood. She heard gossip about love charms and jealous neighbors' curses; she listened to descriptions of violent toddy-guzzling husbands and snooping ancestor ghosts. At one compound today, women were laughing about monks who tried to seduce schoolgirls, plump matrons, even toothless grannies, anyone with a cunt. Lila heard reports about corrupt government officials, a few of whom had gotten caught recently and sent to prison along with the people who'd bribed them for favors. Some of the stories were sad. Army troops had set fire to a peaceful Tamil village up north, causing hundreds of refugees—mostly women and children—to squeeze into the wretched, overcrowded camps. But listen, one old woman piped up: the Tamil Tigers were just as bad—they'd just shot a Tamil nephew of hers because they said he'd cooperated with the government. How could you know which side to trust? Sue shook her head; ever since she'd arrived in the country sixteen years earlier, she'd found the question impossible to answer. Strangely, at several of the compounds she and Lila visited, people they'd known for years didn't ask them in. Instead, they retreated into their houses silently as Sue called to them.

"Last time they gave us fresh cane juice," Lila said, squinting into an empty yard.

"It's like we've gotten some kind of infection," her mother said, and hurried on. "Well, never mind. We'll have more time to visit other people."

Once before, when Lila had taken Zalie with her, some of the people had looked at her suspiciously. Did they fear cats? Or was it that most people were too poor to keep pets and resented a fat, well-fed cat being carried into their homes? Lila never took Zalie with her again. Today some compounds were empty and eerily quiet when they arrived. Windows were shuttered, storage barns cleaned out. At several places strangers were staying. Some of the men stepped into their houses as Sue and Lila passed; Lila could feel them watching from shadowy doorways until she was out of sight. The new women never looked up from their cooking and sweeping. Lila was glad to get back to her house that evening.

She still loved to work in the gardens with Richard. He seemed to be faster than ever at weeding, transplanting seedlings, and clearing scrub brush. When it got too hot, they went for walks along the paths. Once they came to a huge web that a hand-sized striped spider had woven across a sunny spot just after a rainfall. Water beads shone all along the sloping net; Lila pictured strings of tiny festival lights. A pale-pink gecko lizard was squirming around in the web while the spider watched it, motionless on its perch.

The lizard tried to pick up its legs from the sticky web. Its minuscule feet ended in pink baby fingers. Geckos were useful for catching flying insects; that was why her mother never swept them from the walls in the sitting room. Lila liked the transparent lizards that darted along her bed and scampered over her feet like cool squirts of air. The big purple ones with jagged crests and throats that swelled in and out were fun to watch, as well; they stood on stones gazing out of bulbous eyes that swiveled independently in their green sockets. But spiders, too, caught bugs; they had a right to meals. Freeing a lizard from one would be cheating nature. And yet…

"It'd be so easy." Richard touched the web with a stick, making it wave slowly back and forth like a hammock. The spider scrambled closer, then retreated. Finally Richard lay the end of the stick along the gecko's belly. It took hold of the wood with its tiny fingers. Richard flicked it into the air. The lizard went flying safely off into the greenery. "I couldn't resist," Richard said, and tossed the stick away.

Lila smiled, edging past the web. "I'm glad."

They walked on. It was fun hearing him answer questions about exotic things she'd heard about in America: skateboards, book-sized computers with flip-up movie screens, rock music festivals, shopping malls, green-haired kids with pierced tongues, houses with televisions in every room. He was willing to describe these things in the details she demanded, but he didn't seem to enjoy them very much, though he lived right in the middle of them.

"Does Raquel like them?" Lila asked as they walked along.

"Sometimes she says it's all materialist garbage that steals your spirit." Richard grinned. "And sometimes she wants a new seven-hundred dollar stereo for her truck."

"She really has a truck?" Lila pictured one of the long box-car sized Mercedes or Tata lorries that thundered down the main road from Colombo.

"It's just an old pickup—about the size of your Land Rover."

"Do you keep it repaired, so its engine runs?"

"No. Machines and I don't get along so good."

"What color is Raquel's truck?"

"Sky blue. With eagle feathers painted on both sides."

"Long yellow feathers. Like wings," Lila said.

Richard cocked his head. "You just figured that out from my photo, right?"

"Right." Lila smiled.

"Good. I'm involved with enough clairvoyant women as it is."

One afternoon Richard took the twice-a-day bus to the crossroads with her and explored the market while she went to her friend Radha Sharma's thirteenth birthday party. Radha lived in a two-storied white house next to the government health clinic. Her parents had hung the sitting room with loops of gay pink crepe paper and balloons that bobbed frantically along the ceiling in the fan breezes. The television's happy music kept time with its flickering images. Lila wore a new blue dress her mother had made on the sewing machine; Radha and the other two girls had on outfits from Colombo shops. Lila tried not to be jealous of them, and of the presents they brought Radha—a EuroPop CD and an ankle bracelet and a plastic kit of make-up products. Lila's present was a framed painting she'd made of the four-armed goddess Saraswathi playing a lute to her swan on a silver-foil lotus throne.

Mrs. Sharma loved it, and immediately hung it over the glass case where the family's blonde bride-doll was kept on display. The doll wore a fluffy white gown, and over her face was a gauze veil that was never lifted. To Lila it looked like a big petrified child. Sue said such dolls were a modern Hindu custom—they were shrines to childhood innocence. Radha never played with the family doll; right now, she was busy painting her face in the hall mirror. Lila helped Mrs. Sharma blow up balloons. She'd rarely seen Radha's mother wearing anything but her nurse's uniform; today she seemed to shimmer in a blue silk sari. A sprig of sweet-smelling jasmine decorated her hair, and on her arms colored glass bangles clicked and chattered quietly. She looked much more beautiful than the doll.

It seemed strange that only four guests were at the party, especially since the bright yellow cake was big enough to serve at least a dozen people. At school Radha was friendly with the six other Tamil girls in her grade; she must have invited them, yet none had come today. But Mrs.

Sharma, cooing and laughing, got everyone to sing "Happy Birthday," and Radha dutifully blew out the candles. Her mother turned the television's volume up higher.

The three Sinhalese girls gossiped in their own language, so Radha spent most of the party with Lila. She was a quiet girl who couldn't get excited about anything, even Lila's news about Richard's radio and Raquel's winged truck. Radha's new make-up made her cheeks clownish but gave her black-rimmed eyes a haunted look. She kept eating cake with her fingers; crumbs fell down the *choli* bodice of her pink birthday sari. She and Lila lay on the plastic-covered couch and flipped pages of a picture book about Bollywood film stars. Lila wasn't very interested in them but she didn't want to leave Radha alone. Once, when a balloon exploded against the blade of the cake knife, a strange silence fell over the room. Then conversations resumed, sounding louder than before.

The other girls left early, and when Lila saw Richard arrive to pick her up, she jumped down from the couch. Apparently he'd been in the clinic for some time talking with Dr. Sharma. As usual, Radha's father looked about to topple over with exhaustion, though his white coat was crisp and his horn-rims gave him the look of a powerful, important person—which of course he was, as the only physician for many miles around. Radha's eye-shadow dribbled in two wet streaks down her cheeks as Lila left; she kept trying to give Lila the big, expensive film book until her mother gently lifted it from her hands.

"Thank you for the party. Your sari's really nice," Lila said to Radha.

Radha stared up at her mother, and Mrs. Sharma smiled, thanking Lila for her lovely gift.

Outside, Dr. Sharma and Richard kept talking about politics in low voices while Lila scuffled her feet impatiently. Then the doctor sent a servant to stand with her and Richard while they waited at the bus stop. Lila spotted the bulge of a pistol beneath the man's khaki shirt, though Richard didn't seem to notice it. He gazed around at the men laughing as they bargained at the stalls, the women strolling by with stacks of bright folded cloth on their heads, children squealing as they chased each other. He smiled at two ochre-robed monks who glided serenely by as if on little wheels. He leaned forward to smell the bee-buzzing fruit stalls and bullock carts loaded high with fresh-cut lumber. Lila liked the way such ordinary things amazed him; she began noticing them more closely, too. She climbed onto the bus with him and found a seat.

"Such a beautiful island!" Richard said, still staring at the market through the bus window. "Everything looks so peaceful and graceful, but…" His voice faded out.

"But what?" Lila asked.

He shook his head. "Nothing I really understand yet."

Lila had never thought that the market—or any of her life's familiar scenes—had to be *understood* in any particular way. Suddenly she felt a strange silence open around her. It was something like the brief one at the party, but deeper, longer. Years later, she would recall that it was here, on this bus, that it first occurred to her that there were important things she didn't know about this place where she'd always lived—a vast ocean of things—and that they were flowing toward her much too fast.…

"How was your birthday party?" Richard asked.

"I like our parties better," Lila said.

*

She meant the card games she and Richard and Mum and sometimes Papa played every night after supper while the overhead fan whirred (or didn't) and the insects sang outdoors and the quiet concentration was regularly interrupted by someone's voice, often Lila's, saying "Gin!" or "Go fish!" Richard showed her a new game called poker in which you bet match sticks which stood for money. It was risky and exciting. People dared each other; they suddenly got rich or lost everything. At first she went into debt for over a hundred (pretend) rupees but once she caught on to all the games' variations, she was tossing down handfuls of matches and raking them back in across the table with both hands.

"Johannesburg—low diamond in the hole is wild!" she shouted, flipping cards out at people. Another time: "Five card draw, with a roll—ante up!"

One night, her father suddenly stopped playing. He didn't like the bluffing—making players give up by pretending you had better cards than you really did. When Richard bluffed and won, Derek insisted on seeing Richard's cards, though the rules said you didn't have to show them. He even snatched the cards from Richard's hand to examine them.

"I should have known all along!" he muttered. "Damn it, we have to trust each other here—" He stood up from the table and stomped away.

Richard stared at the pile of matches before him. "Maybe I'd better think about cutting this visit short," he said.

"No!" Lila grabbed his hand.

"Don't you dare think that!" Sue said.

Then Sue rushed out into the yard, and for the first time in her life, Lila heard her shouting at her father. Finally they came in, holding hands the way they sometimes did when they went for walks. Derek laughed and said he knew poker was only a game to pass the time—"to poke it along." He sat down beside Richard. "Please forgive my terrible manners. I seem to be possessed these days."

Lila could see how red-rimmed his eyes were; his eyes were squinted half-shut with pain. She was glad when Richard grinned and said "no problem." But her father didn't play poker again.

"Not a gambling man," he said.

*

It was strange that her father didn't like gambling, Lila thought, since his friend, Hans, liked it so much that he'd imported a roulette wheel for the resort hotel he'd built three miles up the road. Lila liked the wheel, which Hans had let her spin as much as she liked in the days when the hotel was new and still attracting guests. But she didn't care much for Hans or his Sri Lankan friends who lounged around the hotel. When they laughed, their gold teeth flashed like the chains they wore around their necks; Mum said they were drug dealers and toddy drinkers. Hans smelled sour like toddy and talked like a big dog barking. When he sped down the road in his new red Jeep everyone had to scramble onto the verges, holding handkerchiefs over their faces to avoid inhaling his dust clouds.

"A red-faced, piss-swilling, shit-eating German communist!" was what Daya called him, informing Lila that German people really did drink huge glasses of foaming horse urine and ate strings of fat, red-brown turds; he'd seen them doing it in a film once. Why a communist? Lila had asked. Because, Daya said, Hans had once been an official in the sports ministry of Germany's communist government; it had collapsed and he'd run off with millions of Deutchmarks. The new German police wanted to arrest him, but for years he'd been bribing Sri Lankan politicians to keep them from sending him back home.

Stopping before the sanctuary gate one afternoon, Hans blasted his horn, waking Daya on his observation platform. "Open now! Your master expects me!" he shouted.

On her way down the driveway, Lila heard Daya cursing in Sinhala as he tried to call the house on the cell phone to get permission to unlock the gate. The next thing she knew, Hans's red car was stopping just in front of her, its engine growling.

"Come! Get in!" Hans called out in his barking laugh. He stood, his sweaty red face appearing above the windshield. He'd chopped his hair so that it bristled all over his head like yellow spines. "Is too hot to walk in zuh sun—mad ducks and Englishmen!" he shouted.

Lila stepped back. "I'm not hot."

Now she could see that the passenger seat was occupied by a small, dark Sinhalese woman. With what looked like one back-handed movement, Hans pushed her into the back seat. He jumped out onto the driveway over the top of his door, pulled Lila by the wrist and plunked her down in the front passenger seat. He jumped in beside her.

"Now we go vast!" he shouted over the sudden roar of the engine. The whole car vibrated. Lila gripped the dashboard. She couldn't help screaming and laughing as they careened up the driveway, nearly tilting over as the little car pitched along the rutted surface. It screeched to a halt inches from the grill of the poor old Land Rover. Lila's forehead struck the windshield, and a wave of terror caught up with her. Then it drifted away, leaving her dizzy. The woman behind her—a girl, actually—was wiping her eyes. But Hans was still laughing, and so the girl managed a smile.

Derek watched him from the doorway. Hans, though he was older than Lila's father, dressed like the young European travelers at the beach hotels—very short trousers and a tank top that showed his enormous sunburnt arms and shoulders. The girl, her pregnant belly bulging under her wrinkled sarong and blouse, was perhaps fifteen. She had chubby cheeks and close-together eyes; her loose black hair didn't look as if it were washed often. She went to sit on the ground under a frangipani bush and turned away from everyone. Hans stepped into the dark of the house, and Derek, glancing around outside (and surely seeing Lila), shut the door quietly. The only time he shut the door with her on the outside was when Hans came to visit.

At the tap beside the front step, Lila washed out a china mug, filled a plastic pitcher, and took them to the frangipani bush. The girl hadn't changed her position; her eyes were focused on the same spot in the grass. Heat swelled loudly around her; the air was heavy with the sweet scent of flowers. When Lila handed her a mug of water, she drank it all down.

"Thank you." She held out the mug.

Lila knew her mother didn't like her to talk to Hans's girl, but she was too curious to keep quiet, and refilled the mug. "What's your name?" she asked.

"Meenu." The girl spoke almost in a whisper. When she'd emptied the mug, water dribbled down her chin.

"I'm Lila." Lila saw a splotch of purplish skin that bulged from Meenu's left eyebrow to her hairline. "What happened to your forehead? Did Hans beat you?"

"Just twice, when he got drunk." Meenu touched her temple. "This one, it's what my father did when I tried to go back home last week."

"My father never beats me. He doesn't beat my mother, either," Lila said. When the girl half-laughed without smiling, Lila could see she didn't believe her. "What did your father beat you for?" she asked.

"He was ashamed. Neighbors said that Hans's friends were fucking me even when Hans was home. But it's not true." Meenu turned slowly toward Hans's battered red Jeep. It stood at an angle on the grass, waiting for its master, catching its breath in the shade of a gum tree. "Everyone believes stupid rumors about me," Meenu said.

Lila nodded. "That's not fair."

"I know. Especially since my father was the one to send me to live at Hans's house in the first place."

"Why?"

Meenu shrugged. "We're poor."

Lila heard Hans's deep laugh from inside the house. "What did he come here for today?"

"Politics. I don't know about these things so don't ask me." The girl drank and held out the mug again. "I don't know why people all take sides, when they didn't used to."

"My father doesn't take any sides," Lila said, filling her mug.

"Maybe. But it's what people think that matters...." Meenu's voice trailed off. Lila felt a chill. She watched the girl lift the mug to her lips with both hands. After taking a sip, Meenu poured the rest of the water over her head. Then, her hair and face dripping, she let the mug fall to the ground. Lila left her staring at her spot in the grass.

*

When Lila arrived at the sanctuary zoo, Zalie was cleaning herself under a big-leafed plant in her cage. The cat's tongue had made a raw, nearly bald patch in her side, but she kept on licking until Lila loosened the wooden peg to open the little gate. Lila wanted to take Zalie out to sit in her lap for a few minutes, but she'd tried that once before. The cat had thrashed violently when she'd tried to push her back inside the cage, scratching Lila's arm, shrieking in a long high voice as if she had turned into some kind of creature that Lila had never seen but had often heard people tell stories about. Lila no longer even considered disobeying the command to keep Zalie confined.

Lying on her side in the grass, Lila managed to pull the bowl out through the cage's wire door, fill it from her water pitcher, and push it back in. The cat widened her big green eyes and rubbed against Lila's arm. Then she tried to nose her way out of the gate. But Lila wedged the peg into place and sat back.

"I'm sorry," she whispered. "I promise you won't have to stay here much longer."

The cat lapped up some water, then began to pace back and forth between the plants and the gate, mewing— always the same insistent rhythm: *mee-aroww, mee-aroww, mee-aroww*, like a car alarm you couldn't turn off. Lila lay her head in the grass, her cheek touching the wire. Eventually she felt Zalie's cool nose push against her skin. The cat lay down and the cries stopped.

"Good kitty," Lila whispered. Zalie softly licked her.

From where she lay, Lila could see the path rise into the rubber trees. Richard appeared among them, walking slowly in and out of the shade-stripes that the trunks made on the ground. He pressed his black radio against his ear.

Sue had explained that he liked to be alone sometimes, listening to his radio or writing in his notebook. So Lila just lay still and watched him. The cat lay still and watched her. Then Zalie closed her eyes and purred.

Lila stood up quietly and brushed herself off. Richard was gone. She had no sketch pad or books with her. But she never stayed bored for more than a few seconds; hearing voices from the house, she ran there quietly as a red Indian, ducked under an open window, and sat against the wall of the house.

From the sounds of their voices, she could picture Hans and Derek sitting at the table inside. She heard Sue come in, set down an earthenware pitcher—clunk—and two glasses—clink, clink. Then she walked out with annoyed footsteps. Hans spoke loudly but his accent was hard to understand, and Derek, who usually had a booming voice, spoke so quietly Lila could make out only some of the words. Evidently Hans had driven to the crossroads to collect Derek's mail along with his own. Derek read aloud from a letter he'd brought, as Sue walked in again. A government official would be visiting the plantation soon, the letter said. Hans and Derek sounded happy about this.

But Sue's voice rose above theirs. "Who is this man? What does he want with us?"

Derek and Hans explained—something about the sanctuary—but Sue still wanted to understand more. Lila knew she didn't like politicians. Neither did she. Officials came to her school and gave speeches about supporting the government and reporting trouble-makers. Usually her father didn't like politicians, either—so why was he trying to explain this one's upcoming visit in such cheerful tones to Sue? Lila heard her leave the room. The men's voices continued—rupees, letters, documents…Lila grew drowsy in the heat. The words fluttered away from her like moths. She rested her chin on her knees and let her eyelids droop.

She woke to hear the Jeep's engine roaring just around the side of the house. Rubbing her eyes, Lila rushed to the front yard. Her parents stood in the doorway as Hans backed his car over the grass. The girl Meenu was in the front seat; she didn't look at anyone. The Jeep nearly hit Richard, who'd appeared from the path beside the house. Now he stood beside the car, shaking hands with Hans, whom he'd met once on his previous visit. Hans spoke to him for several minutes—Lila could barely hear them over the motor's sound. He didn't introduce Meenu. Then he reached out toward Richard's black plastic radio. Lila could tell by Richard's expression that he didn't want to hand the radio to Hans. But he did.

"Short-wave?" Hans asked, yanking up the antenna. For several moments everyone listened to strange staticky sounds. Then, laughing, Hans handed the radio back to Richard, who clicked it off and folded down the antenna. The Jeep lurched forward and careened away.

Lila walked toward the house. It was tea-time—she could see the time in the angle of sunlight through the trees and feel it in the fading warmth of the stone doorstep against the soles of her feet. Richard went inside, stepping between Derek and Sue, who were now looking at each other in silence. Lila ran in after Richard.

"What's going on today?" she asked him. She wasn't used to not understanding things.

Richard shook his head. "I just got here, myself."

Derek flipped the wall switch. The fan started rotating on the ceiling. Everyone watched it pick up speed, the blades spinning, vanishing into a blur. They seemed to blow Lila's question far away.

*

The after-tea cricket/softball match in the front yard started much better than it ended. A brief hard rainstorm had freshened the scent of flowers; Lila pictured their petals opening with little cries like red and white mouths. She squealed as water dripped down her neck from a bush next to which she took her position at deep mid-wicket near the boundary. The crease, where Richard was about to bat, was a patch of bare earth just in front of the gate separating the yard from the top of the driveway. Only one wicket was used; it had no stumps or bails but was just an upright rectangle of tin. If you missed hitting the bowled ball—an old tennis ball—and it flew past you and clanged against the tin, you just had one "strike" as in the American game, and you got two more chances to hit the ball. There were three safe-haven "bases" to stop at if you wanted to; then another person got a turn.

Richard took the weathered brown bat—the same one Derek had used captaining his school's first eleven—and walloped some sixes into the trees beyond the flower beds. Lila had to remind him how to hold the bat perpendicularly with the end almost touching the ground. When bowling, Lila decreed, Americans, such as Richard, were allowed to throw bent-armed. This was added to the official rules with which she'd covered seven pages of a school notebook. Some of the regulations were known to her alone and were invoked only on the field of play as needed. Severe penalties were given for getting the ball stuck among the roof vines. Bonus runs were awarded for hitting a ball into patches of edible berries. Everyone scored high. A partnership seemed to be developing: when Richard bowled to Lila, she hit 3 fours; when she pitched to him, he had 2 fours and 2 sixes.

"Collusion!" Derek called out.

And it was true that Lila wanted Richard to win; he'd seemed sad as she'd seen him walking among the rubber trees. He must be missing his girlfriend, she thought. Whatever the problem was, though, he soon forgot it. Once when Sue caught a ball on the fly one-handed, he gave her a hug that lifted her off her feet. He squeezed Lila's throwing arm and told her she was nearly ready for the "big leagues," whatever they were. Later he shook her father's hand after Derek whacked the ball over the house for a six.

On Lila's turn to bowl, she ran slowly toward the crease, arm rising, then falling as the ball flew. Later, she would wish she hadn't given Richard an easy bounce that let him bat the ball all the way to the potted geraniums beside the front door. He was still running around the "bases" when Lila leaned over the pots. Suddenly she drew back, her hand to her mouth.

"What is it, dear?" Derek called, moving toward her.

Richard stopped running and came over to look.

The awful thing lay in the dirt between two red clay pots—a tiny jar that shone brownish yellow in a slanted ray of sunlight. Its lid was rusty and deeply gouged with strange marks, like writing done with a needle. For his headaches Derek sometimes bought newer jars like this: they contained homemade medicine made from cane syrup and local drugs. But this jar's glass was scratched as if it had been buried and recently dug up. And it contained no medicine.

Lila knew she shouldn't touch it, but wanted to see it more clearly, and she picked it up slowly. Then she just held it as if hypnotized. Richard squatted down and took the jar from her. Deep in her throat, something trapped her voice; she could force no sound out, though her mouth stretched wide at the corners.

Sue ran up and halted suddenly. When she saw what Richard had in his hand, she pressed both fists against her cheeks. "Don't open it!" she cried.

At the same moment, Lila's voice finally burst out. "Richard—stop!"

Too late. He'd already twisted open the jar's lid.

SIX

When Lila drew pictures of Aladdin's lamp, sometimes a turbaned djinn flew out of the spout on swirling purple clouds, or angels like the ones in her school chapel's window floated up to the sky, or recently, a small blue truck with bright yellow wings soared into the air. But this ugly little yellow-brown jar released something she would not be able to draw for many years.

For the few seconds it was open—before her father lunged forward to snatch it from Richard and clamp on the lid—a stench escaped that was sweetish and sickening: like once when a deranged boy outside the schoolyard had furtively stuck his fingers up his anus and, calling her over, pushed them under her nostrils, and afterwards she'd inhaled the stink with every breath until she scrubbed her face with laundry soap. The odor from the bottle was bitter, too: like when she'd seen a workman plunge his shovel into the dirt and strike a buried dog and its stomach burst open in a foul belch of death.

The jar fell from Derek's fingers. He staggered back, turned sideways, and threw up into the geraniums. Vomit dripped from his beard; his eyes went glassy with tears. Then, pressing both hands to the sides of his head, he rushed inside. Sue, Lila, and Richard hurried in after him. Derek fell onto the sitting room sofa under the fan; Sue wiped his face slowly with a wet towel.

"I'm sorry, Papa," Lila said in a small voice. "I was curious."

Derek's eyes opened and his lips bent in an attempt to smile. "Curiosity…" Then he seemed to forget what he was going to say. He reached under the neck of his shirt to touch his *apa nul*, a colored string that people believed could attract good luck or keep curses away. Lila had attached a tiny wooden deer to her string and had saved it in her drawer. Ordinarily she didn't consider the string anything but an old custom, but now she felt she'd been careless not to wear it.

"Where's the fetish now?" Derek whispered.

"It's where you dropped it," Sue said. "We'll get rid of it and forget all about it."

Richard brought a glass of water for Derek. "What *is* the thing?" he asked.

Derek tried to smile. "Just a local superstition."

"It's called *kodivina*. That's like sorcery," Lila said. "Somebody packs the jar with torn flower petals—they're demon offerings. The soft lump was probably rotten meat. It must have been one of the smells—" Her voice choked. She didn't mention the bullet-sized human turd.

Sue took Lila by the hand. "No harm can come—you didn't mean to do anything."

"Richard didn't mean to, either. He didn't know."

"Still, I'm sorry," Richard said to Derek.

Derek was wiping his eyes with the towel. "Nonsense. Just an allergic reaction to something. I'm fine now."

Sue pulled Lila into the kitchen, and beckoned Richard to follow. At the cutting board, she sliced limes with the long chopping knife. "You do it, miss!" She handed the knife to Lila, who cut a lime in two. "Good! Another one!" Sue turned to Richard. "Have a go, Richard—come on!"

He took the knife from Lila. "Is this supposed to help?"

"Well, people think so," Sue said.

Richard whacked a lime, and half of it flew into the air.

Derek, who'd shuffled into the kitchen, caught it in both hands. He was gritting his teeth but managed a smile.

Sue handed Richard a slice of lime. "Wash your hands with this," she said, turning the tap. "You too, Lila."

Derek rubbed his half-lime against his forehead, though from the look in his eyes, Lila could see that it wasn't doing him much good. She rubbed her hands with the lime, then smelled her palms and felt a little better.

"The Indians in Colorado have things sort of like that jar," Richard said as he scrubbed his hands. "Except they're supposed to be sacred."

"These fetishes are the *opposite* of sacred." Sue shuddered.

"All this washing—" Derek said, "it's just to be on the safe side. Knock wood—that sort of thing."

"Okay, what the hell," Richard said, washing his hands. His forehead was creased, his eyes narrowed. Lila thought how out of place he looked here in his jeans, wide-brimmed hat, and an old red T-shirt that said *Cheyenne Frontier Days—1997.*

Sue pressed his palm with both her hands. "Don't worry so much," she whispered.

"Okay," he said. "But you stop trembling, too."

"Me?" She managed a laugh. "We'll chuck the stupid thing over the fence and that'll be that."

"Who do you think brought it, Mum?" Lila asked. "What about that girl, Meenu—Hans's woman? She was alone in the front lawn for a really long time."

"If we even suggest to anyone that she did it, her family will beat the poor kid half to death," Sue said. "If Hans doesn't, first."

Lila nodded. "Actually, Meenu doesn't have any reason to do it."

"Exactly so, Dr. Watson," Derek said. "No motive."

"Right—isn't it more important to find out *why* someone did it?" Richard asked.

"Oh, these things happen here all the time," Sue said. "I suppose someone thinks we're infested with demons or something. People blame their problems on them—love squabbles, low exam results, brush fires."

"And being hungry and poor and scared?" Richard asked.

"Oh, yes." Sue began wiping her blurred glasses on her apron, but it was damp from lime juice and the lenses became more smeared, Lila noticed. Without glasses, her mother's eyes looked watery, unfocused.

"So you just get used to these threats?" Richard asked her.

"What else can we do?" Sue drew a kind of cube in the air with her hands. "If you could look at a space the way the people here do—say, around someone's home—you wouldn't just see a house and banana trees in the yard."

Lila could visualize the air-cube's contents. "Everybody pictures all sorts of spirit creatures flying around," she explained, "like beautiful green-haired *devas* and lost *preta* spirits floating over the grass. And demons with bloody tusks and red-eyed ghosts with stinking, rotten, yellow skin—they swoop around house windows trying to get in. But people say if you drive wooden pegs into the ground around your property you can keep them away—"

Sue winced. "Shhh. What an imagination, Lila!"

"Mum, we've got pegs now!" Lila insisted. "I saw Daya driving them in."

Sue turned to Derek. "Is this true?"

"He wanted to do it. He felt more secure," Derek said.

"There was a man with Daya who said mantras," Lila reported.

"Anyway," Sue continued, "for most people, the world's constantly humming with spirit life. They spend a lot of time making protective offerings and warding off curses with little rituals. Especially now with the war on."

"In times of trouble, witches flourish," Derek said. "That's an expression."

"It makes sense," Richard said.

Derek put down his lime. "Well, I'm going to make a patrol. Have to keep moving."

"Can I come?" Lila asked. This was a question she'd always asked at this time of day, before Richard had come. Now she bit her lip, remembering that she didn't really want to go on patrol; she wanted to play poker or read a book with Richard. Derek gazed at her. Often his bushy beard made it hard for Lila to read his expressions, but not today—his brows drooped, his eyes looked sad, and suddenly she *did* want to go with him, just as always.

"It's probably not such a good idea right now, darling. Till we've sorted out—" he nodded in the direction of the yard where she'd found the jar—"recent developments."

Sue held Lila's shoulder. "It'll be dark soon," she said. "You could clean the lantern globes—"

Lila stamped her foot, her bare heel hitting the toe of Richard's boot. *"Ow!"* She glared up at him, then at her mother. "That's stupid, we've got electricity today."

"In case it goes off." Sue smiled.

"Show Uncle Richard how grown-up you can be," Derek said from the doorway.

"No! Everybody's pretending to be normal and cheerful but nobody is anymore! And you think I'm too young to notice!" She padded noisily across the sitting room and yanked the cell phone from its charger. "Anyway, Papa, you need to take this with you tonight."

"You're right, as usual," Derek said, and came to take it from her hand.

"I charged it for you. It was dead." She ran into her room, slamming her door behind her.

*

Before dawn, Lila peeked in at her father. He lay on his side with his eyes closed. A wet towel was wrapped around his head like a turban. She tiptoed to the kitchen to get his morning cup of tea from Sue, and left it on his bedside table. Awake, he reached out to stroke her hair, then his hand fell to the mattress again.

At sunrise Lila and Richard and Sue got rid of the fetish jar. Lila, taking a newspaper to wrap it in, read cricket scores, gardening tips, and weather reports on the front page. The only mention of the war was an item about some high-ranking Buddhist monks who pledged support for "government campaigns against subversive elements." Kneeling, Sue used the paper as if it were a potholder, folding the edges over the jar without touching it. Lila wrapped twine around and around the parcel, tying knots until Sue said she was sure nothing could get out now.

As they left the house, Lila could hear the trees and bushes still dripping from a night rain. The sun rolled along the edge of the hill like a big orange marble, and Lila saw a whole painting of more marbles on the insides of her eyelids when she squeezed her eyes shut. Beyond the bamboo fence that marked the edge of the plantation, scrub bush sloped away into the jungle.

"Can Richard throw it?" Lila pointed to the newspaper-wrapped package Sue was carrying.

"Good idea. He's got the strongest arm." Sue handed it to Richard. "Just fling the damn thing as far as you can."

Richard weighed it in his hand. "Should I say an incantation?"

"If you know one," Sue said, glancing away.

Lila said to herself a Pali prayer about Lord Buddha, and saw that Sue's lips were moving, too. Richard cocked his arm back. The package flew high into some trees and fell with a faraway thump.

"Gone," Sue said, smiling. "That's over."

"Gone!" Lila repeated.

They started back, taking a long path near the front gate. Lila led the way; Sue and Richard lagged behind, talking in low voices.

"Has Derek trapped anyone yet?" Richard sighted down the false path where two rows of narrowing barbed fence ended in a hidden cul de sac.

"Oh, that thing!" Sue shook her head. "I feel like sneaking out here one night with a pair of snippers."

"It's not exactly a state-of-the-art defense system," Richard said. "And the only escape-vehicle here just lies around gathering moss, while he spends all day playing with wire, wandering around the place."

"He's trying to get away from the terrible pain and worry." Sue's voice sounded scratchy. "He wants so much to be good-natured to everybody, I hate to confront him about things."

"I know. It's taking its toll on you, too." Richard rested his hand on her shoulder.

"This won't go on much longer," Sue said. "Once the government decides about the sanctuary, he's going to be a lot better. Things are going to change."

"You really think so?" Richard stopped.

"Sure. You gotta have faith. Don't you remember, we used to say that?"

"I remember you did. Me, I depended more on action."

"Dear Richard, where did it get you?"

"Well…" He tugged at his hat brim. "Here, eventually."

"Okay. Different paths, same destination." Sue smiled.

Lila paused behind a palmetto, watching through the spiky green flames. Her mother's hair caught a slanting ray of sunlight, looking tangled around her face; when she tried to brush it away, the snarl just fell back over her glasses. Lila saw how skinny her wrists and arms were, how thin she was all over in her faded old blouse and skirt. Unlike most landowners' wives, she did all her own cooking, cleaning, and vegetable gardening—it was all she did, day after day, year after year, almost never leaving the plantation—and now she appeared worn out. If you needed to run up to her and throw your arms around her, she might collapse in a heap of bones and skin and confused hair. Lila walked on, hitting her clenched fists against her sides. Since Richard had come, she'd started feeling strangely restless. Maybe she was seeing things the way he did, too. Maybe it was true: her father was crazy and her mother was…tolled.

She hurried on to the house to see if her father wanted more tea, but when she reached his room, the big bed was empty, its sheets hanging to the floor like collapsed sails. So she went to her room and continued illustrating the book that Richard had mailed her last year. Her painting showed a Navajo warrior who carried a magic arrow that vanquished armies of foes. She dipped her brush into her water glass. Then she paused with it resting on the rim, dripping paint. She watched the drops fall, stared at them as they swirled and curled and twisted in the water and slowly turned it to a murky red fog.

*

Aside from Daya's bad mood—he was pacing his platform, shouting back at some young men on the road who seemed to be taunting him—the next morning was glorious and calm. "Like I remembered it," Richard said, taking deep breaths. Lila remembered how cautiously he'd ventured out from the gate two years before. Now he strode along the road with Lila, and if people stared at him—a white man in a sarong and long cotton shirt and rubber sandals—he just smiled back at them and even said *aaibowan*, which more or less meant "Hello" in Sinhala. The only thing that seemed to slow him down a little was the canvas Air Lanka bag hanging from his shoulder. In it was a fat padded envelope wrapped in white paper and taped tightly. Lila's father had given it to him to take to the abbot at the crossroads monastery. Lila had seen Richard frown when Derek had asked him to carry the parcel for him; he looked uneasy because Derek wouldn't tell him exactly what was inside. Derek wished he was feeling strong enough to take it, himself, he said; but he wasn't, and it really had to be delivered today.

"This will help us to get things settled, I promise you," Lila had heard her father tell Richard. "Then we can do things for the sanctuary—for instance, get that Land Rover in tip-top running condition."

And so Richard was taking the envelope to the crossroads temple. People in twos and threes walked along the road, some women carrying babies, some men pushing bicycles with stainless-steel milk tins or huge bundles of firewood strapped to the handlebars. Hearing a bicycle clatter up behind her, Lila remembered the young man she'd seen on the day Richard arrived, the man riding the handlebars with a bandaged stump for a leg. She half-shut her eyes as the bicycle went by—but it was only a boy with green sugar canes strapped to the rack behind him. She told Richard about the wounded man and how he'd saluted her as if he knew her.

"Radha told me her father had a patient who'd had his leg amputated in the war," she said. "Afterwards, the man thought his leg was aching, even though it wasn't there. It was called a 'phantom limb.'"

"I've heard of that. People think part of them is still where they lost it. They keep wanting to go back and find it."

"That's right." Lila pressed her lips together for a moment. "Did you ever feel that way?"

"Well…no." Richard slowed down, watching her. "But I didn't grow up in a place where I had things like that to worry about."

"I don't exactly *worry* about it. I just get weird thoughts sometimes, that's all."

"Don't we all?" Richard smiled.

Lila let out a sigh. It was nice the way Richard's eyes were such a bright blue in the sunlight. "But you don't have to let those thoughts stay in your mind, you know," she told him. "You can just say, okay, there's a thought, and then sort of nudge it along."

"And it floats away like a leaf in a stream." Richard moved his hand slowly in the air. "That's what your mother says, isn't it?"

"Yes. It's meditation."

"Oh, I know. She's tried to teach it to me. Occasionally I do it, too."

"That's good."

"Yeah, it can be." Richard looked around, then back at

her, as if he were about to say something. Then he just kept walking along, slowly, so that she didn't have to hurry to keep up with him. And so she didn't say anything, either. It was good just to be quiet, sometimes.

The road narrowed and turned like a stream...or, really, like a dusty river bed with banks rising on either side. The banks bordered irrigated paddy fields where rows of women waded in, squatting to gather handfuls of green plants. Their voices fluttered along the mirrored surface of the water; Lila had once drawn the sound in the form of many-colored dragonflies. People's houses were set back from the road. Many were old, the walls of whitewashed dried mud, the painted window frames lopsided, the roofs made of rusted corrugated metal or woven palm fronds. But there were newer houses, too, with cinderblock walls and glass windows and tile roofs. Richard watched a little boy chase chickens from a yard while his mother swept it.

Lila slowed her pace as they passed a new whitewashed house with a Toyota parked in the yard. "Is that what your place looks like in America?" she asked Richard.

"No, I live in a kind of long metal box with cement blocks under it," he said. "Once it had wheels and I towed it around the country behind a truck. I stopped and slept wherever I happened to be when it got dark."

Lila's eyes lit up. "It must have been fun."

"Yeah, sometimes it was." When Richard smiled, creases appeared beside his eyes. "I met a lot of good people. We shared stuff and went into town together at night. I met Raquel like that."

"Was she living in a box?"

"They're called trailers. Raquel was living in one at our camp. She and her family were picking fruit, like I was. It was hard work but it was outdoors, so we liked it for a while. She'd had a year of college, same as me. We were both interested in trees and plants."

"I've got my own flower garden," Lila said. "Mum calls it the Garden of Eden. That's where Christians came from a long time ago."

"I heard about it."

Lila glanced up at him. "Are you a Christian?"

"I used to be."

"Why'd you stop?"

Richard let out a long breath. "Well, when your mom and I were kids our parents liked to dump us off at a holy roller church on Sunday mornings, and then they'd go off places with their buddies. Sometimes they'd be gone all day, and we had to wait around after the services. Those Christians left us sitting under a tree staring up the damn road till it got pitch dark. We weren't dressed up like they were, and they could smell that we didn't take as many baths as they did." Richard shifted the strap of his shoulder bag, staring off across the fields. "Then our parents died and your mom took care of me. Things changed."

Lila remembered her mother telling her how her own mother and father had been killed in a car wreck after they'd been drinking all night at a party. They'd driven off the road into a ravine, and the car had burnt up. That was all Sue had told her about her family. Lila wished she knew more.

"So you stopped going to the church?" she asked.

"Hell, yes." Richard smiled. "Your mother was seventeen then. She rented a room for us in a new town and worked in a restaurant and took courses at a big university. She began doing her meditations. They were the only time she ever stopped working. She used to tell me if people behaved like Buddha said to, bad things wouldn't happen to them like they did to our parents." Richard wiped the sweat from his forehead with his bandana and retied it around his hair. "The university had a kind of Buddhist club. That's where your mom met your father."

"I know. But he wasn't in the club, was he?"

"I guess not, but his friends from Sri Lanka were." Richard slowed down his pace. "It's hard to tell what your father believes, don't you think?"

"He believes in lots of things. Like *devas*. They're little nature goddesses that protect the trees and rivers."

Richard sighed. "I know. Your mom likes them, too."

"Don't you?"

"Sure, why not? But I wish you had more than *devas* to keep you safe here. I don't think they're much good against—" He turned away, narrowing his eyes.

She knew what he'd been about to say. On his radio the night before they'd both listened to a report about a Colombo bank being blown up by a suicide bomber—by a boy not much older than her. The broadcaster said he'd been plump, with prominent teeth; Lila pictured a boar-like demon. The radio had described chunks of concrete falling all over the street, splintered glass crunching underfoot, wounded people being driven away in ambulances.

"Bombs," Lila finished Richard's sentence. "The one you were thinking about was in the city, not out here," Lila said finally.

"So you *can* read people's minds." He smiled at her. "Lila, did you ever think of coming to the States?"

"Not about really going there to live." Lila had listened to his stories and done her best to link them up with the two films she'd seen and the pictures of America in her parents' nature books. "I'd like to see it sometime, I guess," she said. "But what about Mum and Papa?"

"That's the big question." Richard nodded. A motorcycle swerved by; its racket seemed to blow Richard's thoughts away. When the road was quiet again, he said, "Look," and pointed at a house they'd arrived at beside the road. A green metal sign over the door read SPRITE as if that were the name of the owner. The house was actually an open-fronted little shop that sold sweet drinks, snacks, and small grocery items.

"Do you remember this place?" Lila asked. "You got this far after three weeks, last time."

"Do you ever forget anything?"

Lila shook her head. "I miss absolutely nothing. That's what Papa says."

"Do you still like those—what do you call them—chips?"

"Crisps," Lila said, and guided him toward the house with a small tug of the hand. "The brown kind with specks."

"That's right. You want a Sprite, too?"

"Okay."

"Did you know that it's another word for *'Deva'*?" Richard asked.

Lila shook her head. "Do they have them in America?"

"They have the green bottled stuff," Richard said. "I've never seen the other kind. But, yeah, I think maybe they're there, too. At least according to my girlfriend."

"That's good." Lila stepped into the cool shadows of the shop. The air smelled like soap and tobacco. "You can get a cigarette here, too."

Last time, Richard had bought cigarettes one at a time at this shop, lighting them with the glowing end of a hemp rope dangling from the counter. But now he shook his head. "I'm off all drugs," he said. "Except crisps."

He bought two sodas and bags of crisps from the old man behind the fly-specked counter. Then they sat in some metal chairs in the front yard under a coconut tree. The Sprite wasn't really green when it came up the straw out of the green bottle, Lila noticed. She chewed each crisp slowly, even the smallest broken ones, to keep the time from going by fast.

"Nice here," Richard said, gazing around slowly. He'd put the shoulder bag down at his feet, and looked taller without it.

Lila nodded, slurping her drink. The way he chewed made her think the crisps must have been the best thing he'd tasted in years. She noticed that the tree's fronds overhead were making a cool, hand-shaped shadow in the swept dirt yard; she sketched it in her head for later. The old baby bullock cart rumbled by loaded with sacks of rice. In a few days, the driver would put the seats back in, and she'd ride to school in it with her friends all chirping away, and every afternoon they'd stop here to swoop in like a noisy flock of green-uniformed birds and peck the place clean of crisps and sweets. But it wouldn't be as nice as this again. Then she suddenly had another strange thought: Nothing will be as nice ever, so I'd better remember it. Suddenly the shop, and even the busy road outside, seemed terribly quiet, as if all the noises and voices had been sucked away in a big wind. The moment didn't last long, though. She stared at the happy expression on Richard's face and the place filled up with little sounds again like a yard-full of tree frogs waking up all at once.

"I was thinking about what you said about *devas*," Richard said, leaning forward over the table. "Raquel's into spiritual things, too. Sometimes I really want to believe in them."

Lila munched a crisp, watching his face.

"I want to get closer to people who do believe, like Raquel. Like you and your mom." He looked far out the door. "I remember one time a music teacher at my school played us a record of an opera about—well, a kind of *deva*, the kind they used to have in Europe. She was called a *russalka*. And she sang this song about the moon. She was praying to grow up to be a woman, not a water sprite, that was the story, sort of. It was the most beautiful music I'd ever heard in my life. I was almost crying when I heard it. And I thought—no wonder people believe in great stuff like this."

"But you still didn't?"

"I tried, I lit incense and read your mom's books about noble truths. 'Cause everybody believes in something, right? And if you don't, you're on your own completely, and you're vulnerable—you can get hurt bad." Richard looked down into his bottle. "But you can also be vulnerable if you *do* believe. I hate to think that, but I do."

"Why?"

"Because I think about you and your mom and dad. Everybody's been so good to me."

Lila watched his eyes rise and meet hers. She wanted to reach out and smooth the vertical crease in his forehead. Was she too old to do that now? Then it was too late; he leaned back and drank the rest of his soda, smiling at her.

"You're good, too," she said.

"Well, I'm getting by...." He leaned down to pick up the canvas bag at his feet. It seemed to weigh more than before.

"Even if I'm not sure what the hell I'm doing. But then, who is?" He stood up. "You ready to go, Lila?"

"Sure!" She stood up, too. But she wasn't ready at all. Why couldn't she stay here with him all morning, all day? Why did they have to go to the crossroads? An inch of soda remained at the bottom of her bottle. Slowly she poked her straw into it. The drink was too warm, now, like thin syrup, but she slurped up every drop.

SEVEN

As Lila and Richard walked closer to the crossroads, tractors and cars and motor scooters began to pass them, headed for the coast highway. The crossroads was actually a town called Kaduwa, named for the nearest rubber plantation, now abandoned. People hurried by its entrance as if currents of bad air were blowing out from between the old stone pillars.

Lila directed Richard down a neat gravel path that led to the monastery. The *dagoba*—the main temple's roof—shone like a giant white bell in the sunshine; the school's brick building hummed with boys' voices: debates, laughter, chants. All the classroom doors were open onto the yard so you could see the rows of shaved-headed, saffron-robed students seated at their desks inside. They turned their heads to stare at Richard. Under a bo tree, some monks were sitting peacefully with half-closed eyes; others were digging with spades in a flower garden, giving the air the scent of fresh-turned earth.

In the temple's foyer, Lila showed Richard the purple white-speckled feet of Lord Buddha. His ankles ended at the ceiling; Lila had drawn the rest of him rising thirty stories above the roof, his head wearing a wide white hat of clouds. Richard said they were the biggest feet he'd ever seen in his life—which was what he'd said two years ago, Lila remembered. She walked with him up the row of plaster statues depicting Lord Buddha in his past lives— mostly human figures, but a few lions standing on their hind legs with their front paws clasped before them in prayer. On the walls were bright frescoes showing the episodes of the Buddha's life. Most were tranquil: figures seated in green groves, figures trekking through mountain landscapes, figures riding in a boat along a foaming river and in graceful chariots across meadows. Overhead, almond-eyed nymphs in red drapery floated on swirling air currents, their arms reaching languidly down, testing the purity of Buddha and everyone else who might pass.

Richard tilted his head to gaze at the ceiling. "Hi, ladies, I'm back," he said.

Lila smiled, then covered her mouth with her fingers. Would she look like one of the nymphs in a few years, with wide hips and round heavy breasts and hair flowing like dark satin down her shoulders? One of the plumper women was almost as beautiful as Mrs. Sharma. Only a few of the floating ladies were as dark as Lila, though, and not a single one had blue eyes.

"Nothing seems to have changed from last time," Richard said, taking a deep breath. Lila inhaled too, noticing the scent of incense floating out of the deep, old shadows. She'd always loved this place since her mother had brought her here as a child; today its sweet air smelled like childhood; the painted walls and ceiling were, as always, giant windows looking out on the world of the powerful, benign, loving figures who surrounded her life.

She and Richard crossed a courtyard to the monastery's main office. The abbot, a small bald man in a saffron robe, stepped out of a meeting room to his office to greet Lila and Richard. Lila had often met him before, but today he looked different—he was watching her and Richard eagerly, his eyes narrowed, his body tilted. When he pressed his palms together at the level of Lila's face, she smelled the onion-curry breakfast on his fingers. Richard introduced himself and gave him the big envelope from his canvas bag. The abbot showed a great many teeth when he smiled. He squeezed the parcel in both hands.

"Thank you for delivering this—both of you."

Lila glanced away from his smile. Richard took a step toward the outside door.

"I only wish I could offer you tea, but—" The abbot gestured toward the room where people were sitting around a table waiting for him. Two of them, Lila saw now, were wearing dark green military uniforms.

"We have to leave, anyway," Richard said.

"Please give my very best regards to your father," the abbot said. Then, with a swish of robes, he glided back into the conference room and clicked the door shut behind him.

"Whew," Richard said when he stepped back out into the sunlight. "Why do I feel like I need a long bath?"

Lila felt hot and sticky, too. "We can wash when we get home," she said. "Do you want to see my school first?"

He did. They went down another corridor of the temple on their way out of the complex. The hall's air was cool; long tube lights on the ceiling made a high-pitched buzz, lighting another wall of murals. Lila heard bare feet padding on the stone floor behind her. A young monk walked up beside them as if he'd been hurrying to catch up. His head was covered with fuzz; he had narrow, smiling lips. He pointed to one of the pictures.

"History," he said to Richard in English.

Lila and Richard stopped to look. A woman carried an armless man over her shoulder, blood dripping from his stumps.

"Thanks." Richard walked faster.

But the man increased his strides too. In another picture,

an ascetic sat cross-legged on a fire, flames turning his body a blistery red. In another, a pale, nearly naked man stood spouting blood from his chest as dark men set fire to houses in the background. Demon armies decapitated each other ecstatically. When Lila had been younger, these murals had given her nightmares, but when she'd grown older, she'd painted some scenes just as gory herself. She could take disturbing pictures out of her mind and transfer them to paper, where they were just harmless paintings; sometimes the scenes even looked beautiful, in a strange way. Her mother wrinkled her nose when she saw them and asked why she didn't paint the orchids that grew on the trees right outside, or perhaps *devas* or other good life forces. Lila walked on. The monk stopped before another picture, wanting to point something out. A black savage, this one with bulging eyes and tusks like a boar, carried a nearly naked woman off into a forest. The woman's skin was white and her mouth was stretched wide open in a scream.

"History," the monk repeated, pointing at the dark abductor. His lip curled back. "Tamil!"

Richard stopped. "I don't think there were any Tamils here in those times."

The monk tapped the fresco with his forefinger. "Yes. Tamil. Very bad people."

"That's not a person, it's a demon from a story," Lila said, recognizing the figure from her books of *Janaki* tales. Suddenly she was ashamed for having pictured the boy who'd blown up the bank as a boar-like demon.

"This is old myth, not history," Richard said. "Anyway, Tamils don't have tusks."

The fuzzy-headed man looked puzzled and kept silent.

"Do you teach your students this racist horseshit?"

Richard's voice rose. "No wonder they want to go out and torch villages!" Silence. "We don't need a guide," he added.

Lila translated Richard's last sentence for the monk, who narrowed his eyes at her. "I have my orders," he muttered in Sinhala. Though he walked away, he stopped at the end of the corridor to watch from the shadows.

"He's supposed to follow us," Lila whispered as they walked along quickly.

"The saffron secret service." Richard sighed. "It all looked so beautiful and serene here."

"Some of it is," Lila said.

"Some of it always is. That's what makes it all so hard to figure out." Richard walked with his head down, his canvas bag bumping against his side. "Sorry I lost it with that guy inside. It's just that I have to deal with this sort of dark-white thing in the States so much…."

Lila studied his face. "Because of Raquel, you do?"

"We're about the only interracial couple in town." Richard shrugged. "Listen, I hope I didn't get your father in trouble."

"Papa says some of the monks are big frauds. He doesn't really like the abbot, either."

"But he has things delivered to him." Richard glanced around. "Do you know why?"

She shook her head.

"Curiouser and curiouser," he said. This was something Alice in Wonderland said in one of Lila's favorite books; they'd read it aloud to each other. Richard walked down the steps into the sunlight, looking relieved to be outdoors. "Okay, Lila, let's go see your school."

The monk stopped at the gravel path, following them no further, and they continued into the busy market town. It looked a little different to Lila today. Scooter drivers swerved faster in and out of stalls, making more noise and smoke than usual. Merchants and customers were shouting at each other, and people seemed to be in a hurry as they shopped. Was she just imagining this because Richard was tense? Her mother always said Lila was affected too much by the moods of people near her. No, something *was* different, today. She looked around, squinting in the sunlight. Men in green uniforms were walking in pairs with snub-nosed automatic rifles under their arms—that must be it. They looked like the soldiers who had guarded the prison van full of Tamil Tigers. Two unarmed men in uniform watched Richard carefully and moved through the crowd behind him. But when he and Lila arrived at the church, they vanished.

The church, at the far end of the market, was empty. It was a small plain place compared to the monastery and temple; the air inside smelled musty. Lila and Richard's footsteps echoed against the stone floor. Jesus looked lonely, with his arms outstretched on his cross above the altar in the shadowy light. Lila had memorized a few Christian prayers, since the nuns required them, but she'd never given much thought to the religion itself. During the ten minutes the girls spent in chapel every day, they whispered and passed notes while the nuns droned. Now, standing quietly beside Richard in front of the painted plaster figure of Christ, she wondered what it would feel like to have big nails hammered through her hands and feet.

"Why do people do things like that?" she asked Richard, pointing to the poor man.

Richard wiped his forehead with his sleeve. "Probably for the same reason they hack off the arms of ascetics—in the pictures back down the road," he said, glancing in the direction of the temple. "I haven't figured it out yet, myself."

Lila cocked her head. Before Richard's visit, she'd never thought before that there were things about Jesus—or Lord Buddha, for that matter—that you had to figure out. But lately, she'd been trying to do it quite a lot. Overhead, above the wooden ceiling, the church bell clanged in its tower—once, twice...on and on until ten; then it stopped, leaving a reverberation in the air. It had been trying to say something—she could visualize the bell as an open mouth with an iron tongue struggling with a single word—and finally the word came to her: "toll...toll...toll...."—as in a dreary sermon about an island she'd read in English class. It was the same word Richard had used—taking a toll—to describe her mother. Lila was glad to leave.

The two-story brick school was locked for holidays. Through a window, Lila showed Richard her classroom and her desk in the middle of the back row, next to Radha's. "We're always waving our hands because we know the answers. The nuns put us back there so we won't bother the other girls," she said. Richard told her that in America she'd be in a separate class for kids who were especially clever; she wouldn't be shoved to the back of the room. There would be boys in the classroom, too. That made Lila laugh, the idea was so strange; the only boys she knew were the workers' sons, who couldn't read or write, and the young novice monks, who were supposed to stay away from all women, though they whispered things at girls when their teachers weren't watching. Other boys her age went to school in a town down the Colombo highway.

"Don't you ever have friends over to your place after school to play?" Richard asked.

"It's too far. But I play at school. We have netball and badminton—see!" She pulled him around a corner to an open dusty yard. The net was down; the two poles stood naked and forlorn. "And I play cricket every day with Mum and Papa. I read books and draw things."

"Not a bad life," Richard said. "Do you ever get restless?"

"Sure. At least, this year." Lila shrugged. "I don't know why."

Richard pressed his nose against a classroom window. Lila did, too. The seats looked very small today—so did the whole room. She'd been looking forward to going back to school, but now that Richard was here, she didn't want to go back ever.

"The maths teacher is Sister Agatha. Her face's so fat it sticks out of her white head-thing—her wimple." Lila framed her face with the fingers of both hands and puffed out her cheeks. "But she's nice. Last Deepavali—that's the Hindu New Year—she let the Tamil girls have a party and give out sweets their mothers had made for everybody. They were really good!"

"That's nice," Richard said. "A few teachers can give you happy memories."

Memories? Lila looked around at buildings and people as if she were remembering them—though they were right there in front of her. It was a strange feeling.

When they passed a little green-walled mosque, Richard was reminded that he wanted to find the Moslem taxi man who'd driven him to the plantation, so they pushed their way back into the market again, this time into the area where men were repairing cars. Black engine parts lay all over the ground. Mechanics leaned under the raised hoods of cars, clanking wrenches against metal. The smell of oil was everywhere. Now and then an engine roared like a volcano and black fumes plumed into the air.

Richard found the man in the knitted cap. The motors were making so much noise that Lila couldn't hear what Richard was saying. Suddenly the man slipped away. Richard turned around, and there were the two soldiers, waiting to see what he would do next.

"Forget those guys," Richard said, pulling Lila away by the hand. "You've got to help me."

"Okay." Lila picked up her pace. "How?"

"We need to talk to a mechanic about coming out to the plantation to fix the car," Richard said. "That's where you come in—as translator."

"Right." Lila nodded. She was beginning to feel like Harriet the Spy.

At the first little wooden shop that the taxi man had suggested, she asked the mechanic if he could come repair the Land Rover. When he heard the words "Nature Sanctuary," he nodded; he knew where it was. But then he scratched his chin. "Too far," he said finally. "Impossible. I am very sorry." He turned and went into the dark interior of his shop. Two other mechanics said the same thing, though Richard offered them American dollars that made their eyes light up. One man said he'd heard the crazy German had worked on the car, so it was ruined and he wouldn't touch it, himself. Finally a bearded Sikh in an oil-stained jumpsuit seemed to agree, and reached out for the money in Richard's hand.

Richard squeezed the bills. "Tell him he gets half when he shows up, half when the car's running," he said to Lila.

"Okay, no problem," the man said, grinning. He spoke English.

Richard ruffled Lila's hair as they left the row of wooden shops. They could have waited for the bus, but the cement platform near the road was crowded, women with bundles and children packed in under the roof. That would mean, Lila explained, that the bus would be crowded and stop everywhere.

"You'd rather walk, wouldn't you?" Richard asked.

"Yes." She was in no hurry; she wanted this trip with Richard to last. At home, there would be the worry about what her father might say which he wouldn't really mean. And then there was Zalie in the pen, mewing. Lila took the long way around the market, the part where women sold fat, ripe oranges and grapefruit, and bunches of bananas that she could picture as clusters of toucans with long yellow beaks.

Near the end of the market stalls was Kaduwa's little Hindu temple for the Tamils. It was surrounded by a plaster wall and shaggy flowering bushes growing around the gate. Red petals were spilled on the ground around the steps. Lila had been inside with Radha many times; it was just an open rectangular room with a tile floor and a painted plaster statue of Ganesh, the elephant-headed god, sitting on a cement platform at the far end. The flowers people placed at Ganesh's feet always left a haze of sweetness in the air. Worshipers liked to stand quietly and look at the god: women in saris, men in white dhotis or slacks and checked shirts. Ganesh looked back, Radha said, though Lila had never seen his heavy-lidded eyes move. But he did give off a tranquil smile that made you happy to be near him.

"Come on," she said to Richard, stepping up to the gate. He'd like the quiet of the long inner room, the way the light shone through the windows and cast long stripes on the tiles. Leaning on the gate, she reached down to take off her sandals. Then she saw the padlock. Though the gate's vertical bars were rusty and old, the lock was new. It was thick and square, made of heavy steel. Lila gripped the bars in both hands, squinting through them at the open temple door. She couldn't see Ganesh in the shadows, and for a moment, her heart gave a leap in her chest: he was gone, she'd never see him again, all she could do was remember him. The temple's peaceful atmosphere seemed to be trying to flow outside to her, through the old doorway, across the dusty little yard, right up to the gate. Then she heard engine roars behind her, and turned to see two boys on mopeds chasing each other like snarling dogs. She let go of the bars as if they'd turned red-hot.

"It's never locked!" she blurted to Richard.

"Hey, we don't have to go in. What's the matter?"

She shook her head. Then he reached into his canvas bag and pulled out the red bandana he sometimes wore. He put it into her hand and said she should wipe her face with it; her forehead was smudged with the gate's dust. She scrubbed her sweaty skin and held out the bandana to him. He shook it out, rolled it in his fingers, and tied it around her forehead.

"How's that?" he asked.

"Better," she said, and smiled. "Good."

And everything was good for a few long, precious minutes as they walked along the temple wall and across a street toward the clinic. But—such a strange morning!— there she heard a man and woman arguing in the whitewashed courtyard. Richard took hold of her arm to hold her back.

Every day, people waited on benches outside the clinic's door, which stayed open from ten in the morning until long after dark. The clinic was in an alcove behind the Sharmas' white house. Now, though, except for three men too lame to move, the benches there were empty. People stood back as Mrs. Sharma stood shouting at two soldiers in green uniforms. She looked wide and formidable in her white nurse's slacks and jacket. Both the soldiers were skinny and sharp-faced and sullen. To Lila they looked like rats standing on their hind legs, and she was already trying to compose them as a picture when one of them smashed his rifle butt against the bench with a loud thud—then the rats turned into real soldiers again. Now she noticed that the first one was resting his arm in a dirty white sling.

Mrs. Sharma spoke Sinhala with the kind of accent that made Sinhalese girls at school snicker at the Tamil girls when they stood for recitations. They stayed very quiet unless called on. But Mrs. Sharma wasn't at all quiet—she was telling the soldier that his arm could fall off before she would let him carry his rifle into her clinic. No one snickered here. Patients scattered further back.

Mrs. Sharma spotted Lila and Richard on the road, and turned back to the men. "Aren't you ashamed, causing such dreadful commotion in front of a foreign visitor to our country?" She pointed straight at Richard.

Richard started. Then he waved at her, his eyes narrowing. "Hello, nurse," he said in a loud voice.

Both soldiers glared at him. They looked half Richard's age and much smaller than he was, but their expressions were so cold that Lila shivered where she stood. The soldiers had seen foreigners before, though not often in this town; they'd seen too many pale, long-haired, drunken foreign men who wore sarongs and shouted in dissonant languages and vanished into their little palm-frond beach-huts with slim young Sri Lankan girls or with lithe bronze-skinned young boys. The soldiers looked incapable of seeing, or caring, that Richard was older and not a tourist. The soldier without the sling shifted his rifle under his arm. It looked almost like a toy, with only the metal frame of a stock and a small snub of a barrel. But the barrel's muzzle pointed straight at Richard's chest. Lila felt his grip on her arm grow tighter. He was shifting her around behind him. She had no choice but to step backwards.

Then the rifle pointed at the ground again. The two soldiers were talking. The one with the sling handed the other one his rifle and turned to Mrs. Sharma.

"All right, woman," he said. "Let's go."

Then she and the unarmed soldier went in through the door. The soldier with two rifles sat awkwardly on a bench to wait for his partner. Many of the people returned to sit down also. Others stood nearby, murmuring in low voices.

Lila felt Richard's grip on her loosen. Several times she'd seen Radha helping out at the clinic, wearing a white jacket over her sari. Once she had a white cap that she let Lila try on. Lila stared into the door, but again, all she could see were dark shadows. She knew the place wasn't empty, as the Hindu temple had been; she could hear voices and smell disinfectant. But she couldn't see her friend. As Lila looked around at the clinic and the white house—the Sharmas'—beside it, she thought again: I'd better remember this.

Then Richard was talking to her. "What d'you think, Lila—time to go home?"

"Okay." She felt something around her forehead—the bandana—and straightened it with her fingers. Then, as she started walking again, a thought made her break out in a smile, despite how flushed and frightened she'd been a moment ago. I'll write it all down the way Richard does in his notebook—but in drawings: Radha, Mrs. Sharma, Ganesh, all the Buddhas and nymphs, Richard, everybody.

*

The road was quieter and cooler than the market, with the tree branches meeting overhead to shade it, and only the occasional truck or scooter to stir up dust. Lila liked listening to snatches of Sinhala film music that drifted out like long curtains from windows where radios perched on wooden sills. The scents of spicy lunches floated out, too. Children shouted as they ran barefoot across the road. But behind her Lila heard heavy footsteps: another pair of soldiers was following them.

"I had cops trailing me before, but nothing like this," Richard said, glancing back. "Look at those camouflage uniforms."

"My father says they keep track of anybody that isn't familiar here." Lila shrugged the way Richard did. But she really didn't want the soldiers walking behind them all the way home.

"Hans's hotel is just down here. Do you want to see it?" she asked. They'd just come to a branch in the road.

"I don't know. Do you like him?" Richard asked.

"No. Neither does Mum."

"He seems like some kind of desperado."

"What's that?"

Richard grinned. "A *badmash*. Isn't that what they say here?"

It was actually what people in Hindi films called villains, and the word made Hans seem more interesting than she'd thought he was, and she was curious, now. So she took Richard to see his place, hoping to leave the soldiers behind.

Hans had come to Sri Lanka about three years ago, Lila told him, and bought a big house for cash from a local family. Then Hans spent millions of rupees making the house look like a modern hotel, with a fancy bar and restaurant, a casino, tennis courts, a pistol-shooting range, and a big swimming pool. He called the place "Sports Haus." It would be popular, he thought, since so many Germans were coming to Sri Lanka in those days; there were no real resorts along the coast road, only little cabins on beaches and shacks that served bottled beer and charcoaled fish. At first, guests came to his hotel, drawn by curiosity. But they were young travelers without much money; cheap fish dinners were what they really liked, and few of them wanted to trek two miles from the ocean to stay in a hotel surrounded by mosquito-breeding paddy fields. So the Sports Haus had been almost empty of foreigners for several years. Hans spent a lot of time with the toddy-tappers who lived in the valley down the road. They supplied him with home-brewed liquor and, some said, expensive drugs like brown-sugar heroin from Pakistan. It was rumored that he resold the drugs, too. Sometimes he invited the tappers to the hotel for all-night parties where they got into fights and broke things. Then he'd throw them out for a while and spend all day shooting pistols in his range. His neighbors complained about the incessant noise. They also said Hans owed them money. He'd promised them huge wages for work on the place, then given them less money when the jobs were done. Somehow, when they complained to the authorities, the police never investigated.

The Sports Haus was surrounded by a stone wall with a high wrought-iron gate twisted into the shape of an heraldic shield. One of its hinges was broken, and the gate sagged. A flagstone driveway led to a two-story stone building with little castle-like turrets along the roof. On either side were sloping structures of stone, steel, and glass; both opened onto roofed verandahs. Weeds sprouted from between the flagstones. Lila saw no one at the outdoor bar or any of the dining tables. She and Richard both pushed open the gate. Immediately a young man in white slacks and short black jacket stepped out the front door. He recognized Lila from a visit last year.

"The boss is around back," he told her in Sinhala.

"Thank you." Lila watched the man turn, go back through the door, and stand still, watching. She and Richard walked though the verandah between the empty tables with their white table clothes and napkins. Then Lila heard a faint, hollow *pok-pok-pok* sound.

"What's that?" she asked Richard.

"Damned if I know."

They crossed a back lawn whose brown sun-burnt grass brushed against their ankles. In the middle of the open space was a big rectangle of blue tile. It surrounded a long sunken area, also made of blue tile—the swimming pool. The *pok-pok* noises were louder now, echoing up into the yard—hard, insistent thuds, like a person punching something over and over again. Now Lila heard grunts and running footsteps. The pool was empty of water; Hans was running back and forth in the bottom kicking a soccer ball against each end. He'd drawn goal-markers on two walls with charcoal; they were blurred where the ball had smashed into them. He wore only canvas shoes, high socks, short pants, and a thick brown leather belt with an empty holster at the hip. His pale upper body gleamed; his face was red and furious. His bristly yellow hair looked like a helmet that was impossible to pull off.

Suddenly he shuffled to a halt and looked up, his foot resting on the ball. "Allo, allo," he gasped. Sweat dripped off his chin and trickled down his chest. "Come on, play. Richard—you can be goal-keeper, or striker. Which is it?"

"I don't play soccer," Richard said, leaning over. "And I'm not used to the heat."

"Lila is used to it." Hans turned to her.

She took a step back. "I have to go home."

"But you came—that's good. I am grateful. Please, stay."

Richard looked at Lila, who frowned and glanced away.

"We promised her parents we'd be back," Richard said. "We just stopped to see your place."

"Very good, yes?" Hans took a handkerchief from his back pocket and wiped his face. "Real marble floors. AC in all rooms. Full bar."

"Looks great," Richard said.

"Don't go!" Now Hans leaned back to see both Richard and Lila more clearly. "I will give you a cold beer in the bar, Richard," he said. "Lila, for you there is lemonade. And the wheel you like to spin, with the little ball. You will be lucky today."

"Thank you. But—"

"No," Richard said.

"Sure? *Ach*…all right." Hans blinked sweat out of his eyes. "Did your father talk to the abbot yet, Lila?"

She shook her head. Why had he asked that?

"No?" Hans asked, his voice louder. "Then Richard, you saw the abbot today, I think. With a parcel." Hans's lips turned up into a smile, and tiny lines appeared in his cheeks. "You say nothing, so it is true. Good."

"What's good?" Richard asked.

Hans kicked the ball against the wall. "Life is good. Why not?" He laughed. "Tell your father I send to him my best greetings." Hans turned and raced after the ball along the blue tile floor.

Richard gestured toward the driveway, and Lila walked quietly away beside him. The *pok-pok* sounds began again, but faded as they hurried through the verandah. It was a relief to get back onto the road where ordinary men and women were walking. Lila didn't look back at the hotel. She felt better, walking slowly home, but now she was aware of how hot the sun was. It flashed through the tree branches and lit the road like splattering liquid fire. Her dress was soaked through, and Richard, she noticed, was using his forearm to wipe his face and neck. The sound of cicadas closed in around her. At the corner of the main road, no soldiers were waiting. She looked in both directions; so did Richard. Their eyes met, and they smiled.

They walked on. Another tunnel of tree branches appeared ahead, the one before the plantation. At the end of it she saw the steel gate, and searched for Daya on his platform behind its top. Strange—he wasn't there. The gate looked different.

"Something's wrong," Richard said. He sniffed the air.

Now she detected a bitter scent: like fireworks—burnt gunpowder. She and Richard both started walking fast around the bend. The gate was a patch of bright green, but its lower part was mostly hidden by a crowd of men and women. The dirt on the road near the gate was scorched. Rising from the ground and up the middle of the gate was a black splotch where the paint had been exploded away. The steel was dented, and the lettering was nearly gone.

"What happened?" Richard shouted, rushing forward toward the crowd.

They all stepped back, going silent, staring down.

Lila asked the same question in Sinhala. Most of the men shook their heads, muttered that they didn't know, they hadn't seen anything. Then one old man pointed to a jagged piece of metal. It had once been a square box; now its sides were twisted like scraps of paper blackened in a fire.

"I think someone filled a tin with gunpowder and set it off," Lila said.

Richard stood closer against her, his arm going round her shoulder. When he tried giving the gate a shove, it wouldn't move. "Daya!" he shouted.

Lila shouted, too. "Papa! Mum!"

Silence. Then the murmuring started again from the people staring at the gate. Lila recognized some of the men; they'd once worked for her father. Now their faces were dark and expressionless; they didn't smile to greet her or even look up from the road. Finally Lila heard her name being called.

"Mum!" she cried out.

The gate swung open a crack. First Daya, then her mother edged through. Her hair was unpinned and tangled on her cheeks. Dropping to one knee, she pulled Lila close.

"Oh Lila—it's all right, dear."

"Who did this?" Lila asked, her voice muffled against Sue's blouse.

"Just somebody with a grudge—I don't know—"

"Is Papa all right?"

"He—he's not hurt. No one's injured. Everything's okay." As she stared up at Richard, her eyes grew wider.

He stepped forward. "Sue—"

She shook her head hard. "Let's go up to the house, Richard."

Richard rested his hand on Lila's shoulder. "Come on, Lila. Walk with us. Nice and slow," he said, glancing around. People were crowded around the opening of the gate.

Lila's rolled bandana had fallen at an angle over her eyes. Reaching up both hands, she straightened it across her forehead. The murmuring grew louder behind her. She looked straight ahead and walked up the slope of the driveway between her mother and Richard, wondering what she would find at the top.

EIGHT

From where Lila stood on the drive, the house looked overgrown and empty. Greenery hung down its roof and walls; its windows were open with the curtains all sucked inside, as if it were a shell of a house whose square holes would soon be clogged with leaves and vines, too. Though she hadn't heard the explosion, an echo seemed to reverberate in the air around her. She ran toward her father as soon as she saw him sitting at a sideways tilt on the front step. When he spotted her he stood up on wobbly legs; his eyes were shiny.

"You're all right, Lila!" He hugged her against his chest, his beard tickling her forehead.

Lila pressed her cheek to his sweat-soaked shirt. "What happened, Papa?"

"Only a stupid prank. Please, don't worry."

Sue and Richard helped Derek to walk inside and eased him down onto the sofa. "I'm sorry for all this commotion, just when you come." Derek, blinking hard, looked up at Richard. "You must think that people are out to frighten you away."

"No," Richard said. "I don't think that."

"Good." Derek settled back against a pillow, half-closing his eyes. The skin of his forehead was lined with indentations that seemed to be made by tightly drawn transparent wires. "It's us they're trying to frighten—on two fronts," he said. "One is…spiritual: that fetish jar. The second is the political front—boom!" He raised both hands to describe the explosion at the gate.

"Who's doing this?" Richard asked.

"Always we hear—Tamil Tigers." Derek shook his head. "Everything bad is because of Tigers. But I think that's utter rot."

"Of course it is," Sue said, turning to Richard. "A lot of landless people are coming down from the refugee camps in the north. Families are just looking for someplace to settle."

"I've seen them on the roads," Richard said.

"This has been going on for years—people trying to get into the plantation," Derek said.

"But there's already people here," Lila explained.

"Lila's right." Derek's eyes fluttered wide open. "We owe our workers enough space for them to live. They depend on us, as we do on them. The plantation can only support so many people."

Richard sat down beside Lila. "What about the sanctuary, though?"

Sue and Lila also turned to Derek. He sighed. "The eternal question of land use—wildness or cultivation? There must be room for both!"

"There *must* be," Sue repeated. She brought a pitcher of water and poured glasses for Derek, Richard, and Lila. "Anyway, Richard, there've been a lot of government peace initiatives. They're bound to have an effect soon," she said.

Lila drank her glass of water. She wasn't sure what "peace initiatives" actually were, but she'd heard the words on the radio so many times while helping her mother in the kitchen that she assumed they must mean something good.

"There are political negotiations, military cease-fires, all sorts of meetings," Derek said.

"According to my radio," Richard said, "the talks are breaking down."

"Perhaps, but they'll start up again. This has been going on for years, too."

Lila saw Richard cock his head. But Sue leaned forward with her pitcher of cool water to refill his glass. "You know," she said quietly, "Chandrika really has everyone's attention. She's very determined."

Mrs. Chandrika Kumaratunga was the Prime Minister; she was known by her first name, at least by people who supported her. Lila had often seen her on Radha's television screen—a broad-faced middle-aged woman with big sad eyes who tried to smile when she talked to the people. She often spoke about new peace initiatives…which would never interfere with "sweeping military objectives" and other things that Lila couldn't remember. Chandrika was the widow of the last PM, who had been assassinated in Colombo. Her father, too, had once been a prime minister. And he, too, had been murdered. In all her history classes, Lila had never heard of leaders in one family being killed like this. On the television she occasionally saw grainy maps of countries like Yugoslavia, Israel, Northern Ireland, Congo—places where political leaders got shot or blown up. A president of America had even been assassinated just before Richard and Sue were born, so Lila guessed she shouldn't think it so strange.

She didn't like to watch Radha's television because of these news broadcasts. The other programs were more cheerful—Sinhala film clips, lots of cricket matches, endless music videos from India and Hong Kong—but they were boring, and in their own way almost as distressing as the news. People moved more and more frantically—shooting guns out car windows, running after balls, dancing with their arms flung back and their pelvises thrust forward like garishly painted mechanical toys stuck at high speeds. They did make you forget the news broadcasts; that was good. But they were like strange dreams you could never wake from.

"Richard, we have our own peace initiatives, right here in the sanctuary—on political and spiritual fronts," Derek was saying. "First, the government's going to help us."

The vertical lines appeared in Richard's forehead, but he said nothing.

Derek smiled, tilting sideways on the sofa. "Better we wait to talk about this, though. Until everything is signed on the dotted line in a few days. Secondly..."

Lila leaned against Richard, restless. She badly needed to get her pad and draw something—anything. Mrs. Sharma and Radha—yes, she'd draw them plump and smiling in white nurses' uniforms, and they'd be floating on light green air currents like the ones on the corridor ceiling at the Buddhist temple.... But now her father was asking her something, and she had to sit up straight.

"Lila, do you remember Silindu's ceremony last year?"

She nodded. "When he was so sick," she said. Silindu, one of the workers whose plot of land was behind the rubber trees, had lain in a fever on his mat for weeks, speaking in a strange high voice. The voice belonged to a demon, his wife insisted; an angry neighbor had sent it to him after a land dispute. And so a drummer and two dancers had come. Becoming possessed themselves, they screamed at Silindu's demon and dragged the man to his feet so that the demon would have to dance with them. When Silindu finally collapsed onto his mat, his fever was gone and his voice was normal again. The visitors, who'd tempted the demon out of his body, carried it away triumphantly in a tightly fastened straw basket. Lila had glimpsed several such ceremonies, on a smaller scale, while visiting workers with her mother. A person who flushed demons from a victim was like a village doctor. Radha's father occasionally referred his patients to one when they didn't respond to his treatments. Spirit practitioners sometimes referred their patients to Dr. Sharma, too.

"Some of the most prestigious exorcists," Derek announced, "will be coming here, if all goes as we hope it will."

"Then can we let Zalie out?" Lila asked.

"I hope so, dear," Derek said. He turned slowly to Richard. "Not that I take this sort of sorcery seriously, you have to understand," he said. "A British education made me believe in science. Our schoolmasters told us that the *devas* and so forth are only for peasants and low-caste, ignorant people. Even my parents taught me this. But when my father got sick, and the hospital couldn't help him…" Derek smiled briefly. "At any rate…once that fetish jar was planted here, word got out that we've been…be-demoned. We're vulnerable. Now everyone is waiting to see if we will make a show of strength against the curse. And so we'll have to."

"Okay," Richard said, glancing away.

"It's sort of like some of those *Janaki* stories," Lila said. "Men will come and act them out."

To Lila, this seemed like an interesting, even exciting, plan…why, then, didn't her parents look more enthusiastic about it? They must be still worried about the explosion at the gate, since they'd been here to hear it. Her mother's hair was tangled over one side of her face, her glasses smudged, and she sat slumped forward, inches from Derek but seemingly unable to reach him. Her face was lined, tired—tolled, Lila thought. And her father was leaning precariously sideways on the couch. Sweat—or tears—rolled down his cheeks; his eyes were two half-moons, completely shut now. The invisible wires were drawn even more tightly around his forehead.

Nothing more was explained or decided. Everyone sat still, as if listening for something.

*

Even in the hottest seasons, breezes used to blow through the open doors and windows. During power outages, the air moved through the house and stayed fresh, but recently, Lila thought, it was slowing down; she felt it tightening around her, then twisting away and leaving her off-balance. Nothing happened except the heat and quiet increased. Her father lay on his bed, or patrolled the fences with Daya when he could; her mother stayed in motion, cooking, cleaning, gardening, stopping only to meditate.

Since the explosion, Lila was told not to leave the plantation. She felt penned in, though not quite bored. She visited Zalie and helped her mother and worked with Richard clearing a patch of land. Occasionally he glanced at engine noises at the bottom of the driveway; he said he hoped the Sikh he'd spoken to in the market would arrive to repair the Land Rover, but no one came. He and Lila listened to American music on his short-wave radio—he liked noisy operas and twangy country-western music—while he slashed away with his machete and she tugged at vines that grew along the ground. She liked to reel in yards and yards of them until they lay all around her like tamed green feathered serpents. He paused now and then to watch creatures he unearthed—swarms of ants, lizards, millipedes, the occasional scorpion or rat or green snake. He pushed them gently away with the side of the machete blade if they didn't scamper or slither off on their own.

"Are you going to come to the ceremony?" Lila asked him as they worked.

Richard squatted down on his heels so that his face was level to hers. "I don't know. Your Mum seems afraid to talk to me about it, and your father won't say much, either."

Lila looked at him sadly. "Maybe because you don't believe in it."

"Do you, Lila?"

What a strange question. Maybe he meant, did she think the *aduras*, the men who did the ceremonies, were honest. "Some of the exorcists are scoundrels," she said. "You have to know the good ones. That's why people ask the monks' advice sometimes."

"The *monks* advise them about this stuff?" Richard shoved his machete tip into the ground. "I thought the Buddhist clergy were against demon worship."

"Oh, they are. Our teacher from the monastery, the one who helps us with Pali texts, he says it's all ignorant pagan nonsense," Lila said. "But one of my girlfriends told me she saw this teacher once dancing in a trance. It was in a little temple in the countryside."

"So you think—?"

"I don't know!" She didn't know what to say. A jagged streak of light slanted down from the tree branches into her face. "It's too hot to work outdoors today. If you get sunstroke it can make you crazy." She stomped off toward the house, trailing a leafy vine.

Later, she lay on the sofa listening to Richard and Sue talk about America at the dining room table. They spoke about freezing their fingers as they shoveled manure in a dismal old barn, warming their hands on the steaming flanks of cows to keep frostbite away. They remembered fleeing up and down stairs as their father lashed out at them with a belt in his drunken rages.

"When I got here," Sue said, "it seemed like the most peaceful land in the world. Everything was just as beautiful as Derek had said it was."

"You thought beauty caused peace," Richard said. "So did I, once."

"Beauty, spirituality, peace—planting, watching things grow, harvesting...." Sue shut her eyes, her chin resting on her palms. "Half my life, I've believed...."

Here Lila shut her eyes, too, but then she dozed off and missed the rest of the talking.

In the evenings, she still played cards with Richard and Sue. But once, when Richard asked her if she wanted a game of poker, she thought of her father lying on his bed with tears running down his cheeks; then she said, "I don't gamble," and went to her room. She wasn't angry with Richard exactly; it was just that he made her think about things that she'd never thought about before.

For instance, after he and Lila had listened to his radio's broadcast about the boy who'd blown up the bank in Colombo, a picture of the boy got stuck in her head and wouldn't leave her unless she drew him. The radio had called him a "suicide bomber" so Lila knew he was dead. Since he'd died unnaturally—violently—he wouldn't achieve *samsara* and would have to wander as a *preta* between the earth and Heaven. Lila painted him hovering restlessly above the bank's ruins. The sky behind him was fiery red and below him lay chunks of concrete that were the same scorched blackened color as the gate after the explosion. Soldiers in camouflage uniforms were doing a frantic video dance in the ruined streets. Several of them raised their rifles and tried to shoot the boy out of the sky. Did bullets hurt as they went through a *preta's* body? Lila was pretty sure they did. She shouldn't feel sorry for someone who had blown up so many people, but she couldn't help it—the boy was so young. And the Tiger guerillas might have threatened to torture people in his family, maybe his parents or even a little brother or sister, if he didn't do what they told him to. On Radha's television she'd seen a captured guerilla admit that the Tigers did that. But Radha said the government troops had probably tortured *him*, the guerilla, to make him say that. They used electric wires and burning cigarettes and worse; one of Rahda's cousins had gone insane after the army had finished with him, and he'd never even *been* a terrorist.... Lila got a headache trying to figure this all out; it didn't go away until she started more paintings.

Finally she forced herself to do her school assignments. Holidays were coming to an end soon, as her mother kept reminding her. "I'm memorizing a poem!" she shouted, when Sue asked her why she was staring off into space. "Leave me alone!"

"Look who's grumpy!" Her mother ran her fingers up Lila's spine. This usually made Lila giggle, but today she squirmed away, scowling.

Maybe she was a little bad-tempered, but her mother was touchy, too, scrubbing the floors and waxing all the furniture, just because somebody called the "Assistant Minister for Ecological Affairs" was supposed to come to the house. "We don't want to look like—well, trash!" Sue said, making her rag squeak against a windowpane. Her eyes seemed blurred, as if she were groping blindly with her hand, automatically wiping everything that got in its way.

*

One day after a brief rain had cooled the air, Lila went with Richard to collect the mail at the gate. The workers had painted it bright green again so that you could barely see the indentation in the metal. Stenciled black English letters, even bigger than before, announced *PRIVATE: NATURE SANCTUARY*, with the same words underneath in rounded Sinhala script.

Hans used to pick up the family's mail at Kaduwa in his Jeep, but Sue suspected he was losing it, or reading it, so now one of the plantation workers fetched it on his bicycle every Wednesday. Daya, bored on his watch-platform, swept the dirt smooth in front of the gate, leaning over with his short-handled broom. The worker's bicycle came into view out of the tunnel of tree branches.

"Babahami!" Lila shouted, waving to him. Like her mother, Lila knew all the workers' names; she'd grown up with them and their children. Each week, as Babahami's bicycle clattered to a halt, she could tell from his expression if he had a blue aerogramme from America, from Raquel for Richard. She liked the way Richard's face relaxed into a grin when the letter appeared in Babahami's hand. Richard always read the letter, or most of it, to Lila; she felt she was getting to know Raquel pretty well.

In past letters, Lila had learned that Raquel had gotten a B+ in an accounting course at the community college and an A– in biology. She planted over a hundred new seedlings for the nursery where she and Richard worked. At a powwow, her father had tied a powerful white-tailed hawk feather to her braid, and it made her dance so much like her mother had that her father saw her mother in a dream, and all weekend he didn't take a single drink. Sometimes Raquel baby-sat a neighbor's boy who was retarded and ate all the sugar in the pantry while she was reading, but his mother paid her back with a chicken though Raquel hadn't asked her to. One of her horses—she and her two uncles owned seven—had to see a vet who charged so much she couldn't pay all the electric bill. The school was giving her little brother a hard time so Raquel went there for a "nice chat" with the teacher but ended up telling the bitch she'd clean her damn clock next time she got on the kid's case. She lost ten pounds and could get into those black jeans Richard liked so much…. (Here Richard cleared his throat and skipped ahead.) She made a down payment on an amazing stereo for the truck. But sometimes she turned it off when she was driving home from work and stopped beside the highway to watch the moon rise, and if she opened up the windows and sat very still she could hear the snow falling all over the meadows. She missed Richard a lot.

Today Richard got not only a blue letter but a postcard. "For you," he said, handing the card to Lila.

"Me?" She never got mail except from Richard, and he was right *here*. This postcard showed a painting: a dark woman with long braids leading a horse toward a white-topped mountain. The caption said, "Sakajawea: Indian Guide." She turned it over. *"Hi, Lila,"* she read aloud, *"I feel like I know you, R writes about you so much. He says you are winning all his money in card games. I hope you can come visit here so I can meet you—Raquel (R's lady). P.S. I have a cat named for a flower, too. Daisy. How bout that?"* Lila looked up. "Does she really want me to visit?"

"Sure. So do I. I've been waiting to ask you again till your father's better."

Lila looked at the painting side of the card again. "That must be snow on those mountains."

"Right."

"I'd like to see snow...." But when Lila gazed up the driveway leading up to the house where Mum and Papa were, and noticed the little purple trumpets in the bushes and the palm trees bent against the sky, it was hard to picture herself anywhere but here. "If I left, could I ever get back?" she asked, her voice low. "Would Mum and Papa still be the same? And Radha and Mrs. Sharma and Daya?" Lila turned the postcard over and over in her hand, studying it as if it were a puzzle. "Or would they change while I was away?"

"You've been thinking about this," Richard said.

"Everything changes, I know," Lila said. "Permanence is *maya*—not real."

"Is that what your Mum says?"

Lila nodded, staring up at the palm trees again. "And Lord Buddha."

"But he doesn't say you have to make up your mind today, does he?" Lila shook her head. "And Raquel doesn't need an answer right away, either. She's just saying she'd like to meet you, if it works out."

Lila let out a long breath. "Who's that?" Showing him the postcard again, she pointed to the woman with the horse.

"Sakajawea? She showed some white explorers around the country. They didn't have a clue about what to explore or how to live. But she knew where everything was and

what it was for and how it would help them." Richard
smiled. "Raquel chose that card carefully. And not just for
you."

Lila glanced at the blue aerogramme in Richard's hand.
"What about your letter?"

But now Richard was staring out through the gate at the
road. Something was coming, pushing a noisy roar ahead of
it. Then engine rumblings expanded fast as two fat
motorcycles swung out into the sunlight and skidded to a
halt, making ruts in the soft dirt in front of the gate where
Daya had been sweeping. From the back of each cycle a
soldier jumped off, pointing a snub-nosed rifle in a slow
semicircle, though no one was on the road except an old
Tamil lady carrying a sun-umbrella. The two drivers
straddled their cycles, their black-gloved hands squeezing
the handlebars, making the engines sound furious. They
wore round helmets with plastic shields that hid their faces,
and for a moment Lila saw them as giant bluebottle flies.

More people appeared, attracted by the noise. They
climbed up the slope that bordered the paddy fields and
stepped out of the little houses down the road, but they
kept their distance, watching. More noise approached—this
time a heavy car that also stopped in front of the bright
green gate. The motorcycle soldiers shouted down the road;
people stepped backwards as if they'd been prodded.

"What do you want?" Richard asked.

The soldier gave him a long look. Then he turned toward
the gate. "Open! We have come!" he shouted to Daya in
Sinhala.

"*Who's* come?" Lila asked him.

The soldier didn't glance at her.

She heard Daya's voice from the platform—"Opening!
Opening!" He leaned out, his cell phone pressed against his

ear, and shoved the gate. Already ajar, it swung inwards until there was room for the car to get through. It was a stocky, gray vehicle with a heavy chrome grill and a small flag drooping from a stick on the right fender. Its windows were so black that Lila couldn't see anyone inside. The car rolled through the gate, then stopped again.

Now Lila could see her reflection in the shiny side door and the black glass. She looked much taller and darker than she'd ever thought of herself. Her eyes were strangely pale. Then the top of her reflection—her forehead, her face, her neck—began to peel downward and vanish. With a humming sound, the window slowly descended.

NINE

A head—not her reflection—appeared in the car window as the glass stopped gliding down. All she could see in the window now was a man's round face with a tight-lipped smile.

"You must be Derek's daughter, Lila," the face said.

Lila neither replied nor nodded; she didn't like this face knowing her name.

It poked out the window. "And this is your Uncle Richard, I believe."

"That's right." Richard stepped beside Lila. The vertical indentation deepened in his forehead.

The man in the car spotted Daya and spoke to him in Sinhala: "Do you expect me to drive up this rutted river-bed? Go tell your master I'll wait for him here."

"Yes, sir." Frowning, Daya started up the drive, his pace deliberately slower than usual.

Lila felt air pouring out the car window like sour, chilled breath. "My father's sick in bed. He can't walk down here."

The man looked up the drive. "I didn't know. Well, I'll drive him back when we're finished. While we talk here, the AC will be good for him."

"No, it won't—" Lila word's were lost in the growl of a motorcycle as it rolled up to the car. Through the gap in the gate, she saw that more people had come; they were still keeping their distance. The men and women looked angry, frightened, curious, their bodies poised to dart off at any second.

"We'll keep the girl here, send the uncle up to the house," the man in the car said to the motorcyclist. He turned to Lila.

For the first time she noticed a mole on his upper lip hard as a mouse turd; it bounced when the lip moved. "You're very welcome to sit in here with the AC while we wait for your daddy," he told Lila in English. Lila shook her head.

"She'll stay out here with me." Richard faced the car window. "I thought this was a friendly visit. The family's been looking forward to seeing you."

"Oh, very friendly, I assure you—" Now the door swung open and a body as well as the round face appeared. The man wore a dark suit, open shirt, and no tie. His shoes were shiny black. He suddenly stepped past Richard.

"Derek!" He raised his arm in the air.

Lila's father approached the car slowly and stiffly. He wore a pressed white shirt that matched his slacks. His hair was combed straight back from his forehead the way Lila sometimes drew ocean waves rising. In his beard his teeth were visible, gritted but smiling.

"Welcome, Minister," he said in a booming voice. To Lila he said more quietly. "Take Richard up to the house, Lila. Mum's making tea for us all."

"I don't want tea," Lila whispered.

"Could you go with her?" Derek asked Richard, his smile tightening.

"All right," Richard said. "But are you okay, Derek?"

"Of course!"

As Lila walked up the drive beside Richard, she looked back over her shoulder to watch her father step into the car with the minister. The soldier shut the door with a click, and the window glided back up, shiny as black marble.

At the house, the sound of the car motor receded until it was only background—always there, like a faint toothache, but intermittently ignorable. Lila longed to hear the usual twilight twitter of birds, but they were keeping silent, as if waiting for normal life to start up again, too. Sue had taken a tray onto the front steps and given Daya a cup of tea. Though she told him to sit down, he continued to pace. Richard and Lila took cups from her and sat on the steps.

As she waited, Lila turned her postcard over and over in her hands, reading the message so that she could just about hear Raquel's voice talking to her. Lila pictured herself as the red Indian guide, speaking to her horse in a low voice, climbing onto its back so she could ride up into the snow on the mountain. Lila had seen horses once in a parade in Colombo, their hooves clacking against the tarmac like teams of hammers. Riding a horse didn't look difficult.

"I made a cake for the Assistant Minister," Sue said. "But the hell with it, we'll just eat it ourselves, and everything will be fine."

"I'm not hungry—" Lila started to say. Then she saw Richard raise his eyebrows at her. "Oh, coconut cake. Thanks, Mum." She took the plate Sue handed her.

"It's good, Sue," Richard said, his mouth full.

Daya was also munching a piece, white coconut bits stuck in the corners of his dark lips. He strained to see down the driveway. "There were too many people around the gate," he grumbled, wiping his mouth. "They want to look at the great man's elephant." He meant the big gray car. "Some of those people don't know they're going to have to clean up the piles of dung it leaves behind."

"Daya—" Sue frowned.

"But many of the people know that politician, and they hate him," Daya said, as if to himself. He fingered the two brass buttons left on his khaki jacket. "Everyone says he takes money from both sides...."

"You can't listen to rumors," Sue said.

Daya moved down the steps. "I am going to make sure the gate gets closed when he leaves—" He glanced at Lila "—just to keep the fruit thieves from slipping inside."

Lila watched the old man pad across the yard. Sue looked at her watch. She hadn't touched her cake or tea.

Richard turned to her. "I heard the BBC today—from the Madras relay, I think. The guerillas are coming down the coast from the north. The army isn't stopping them. Some soldiers are running off into the bush."

Sue rubbed her forehead; her glasses went crooked on her nose. "I don't know why you should automatically believe the BBC—?"

"And Radio Nederland. Their broadcast said about the same." Richard sat forward. "The government's just lost another town, Perinawiya. That's only about a hundred miles from here, I looked it up on Derek's map," Richard said. "Meanwhile we're setting up a park to protect wild deer and rare orchids."

"I wish you wouldn't be so damned negative. Life has to go on." Sue raised her teacup to her lips; its heat fogged her lenses. "Lila, dear, see if you can spot your father on the drive. Go on."

Lila gladly moved down onto the cricket pitch. When Richard and Sue argued these days, she preferred to keep her distance. Before Richard had come, her curiosity always got the better of her and she stayed close by to hear grownups' fights. Her mother and father argued mostly about things that could be decided fairly easily—crops, money, workers' problems. But Sue's and Richard's disagreements were quieter, never finishing. She looked at her watch. Twenty-one minutes had gone by since Papa had gotten into that elephant car. She gave the metal cricket wicket a clang with her foot, sending it skidding against the nearest fence post. She ran from the crease to the first haven—"base"—then to the second one by the pile of coconut husks, then to the third one near the garden stump. Instead of running to "home base," she climbed the stump to take another look down the hill. Thirty minutes....

Now she spotted her father's white shirt as he slowly walked up the driveway. "He's coming!" she shouted over her shoulder, and ran toward him.

Derek smiled and put his arm around Lila's shoulders. He moved stiffly, his head up, eyes glassy bright. As soon as he entered the yard, though, his legs started to wobble. Richard and Sue rushed to him; they half-carried him up the steps of the house and into the sitting room.

"Why didn't that man drive you up here in his car?" Sue asked. "I don't understand this at all!"

"I said—I'd walk. Can't—let them see—your troubles," Derek said, settling back onto a couch. "Not even your friends."

"Friends?" Richard asked.

"Look!" Derek pulled an envelope from the pocket of his shirt and waved it in the air. Then he handed it to Lila. "Victory!"

She stared at it: she'd never held such smooth heavy paper in her hand before. "Shall I open it?" she asked. When her father nodded, she pulled a letter from the envelope. At the top of the page was a heavy black seal.

"You see?" Derek said, staring up at Sue. "All—all those inquiries I wrote, those blueprints, those applications."

"They paid off!" Sue wrapped her arms around Derek, pressing his face against her chest. "You've done it, darling!"

"Shall I *read* it?" Lila demanded. When her mother said to go ahead, Lila smoothed the letter out on the dining room table and spoke in a loud official voice, trying to sound like the government bulletin-reader on the radio.

"Dear Mr. Gunasekera: In view of your generous donations to our party's Natural Heritage Fund—"

"Where'd you find any money for that?" Sue asked Derek.

"Friends, family in Colombo," he said, sitting up. "Read on, Lila."

"Your property has been designated a National Trust Sanctuary, in which hunting and the taking of wild plants is strictly forbidden by anyone not already dom-iciled within the para—para-meters." Lila drooped her tongue sideways out of her mouth and crossed her eyes. Then she went on. *"You are guaranteed the protection and support of the government in keeping this area free of intruders, and we welcome your suggestions for projects—"*

"You've got drawers full of project proposals," Sue said.

"Five years' worth of them," Derek nodded slowly. He looked out of breath. "In fact, most of them are already on file with the Ministry. I wonder what happened to them."

"You can send in copies." Sue took his arm. "The important thing is the government support. Will the Minister be sending guards?"

"I suggested guards." Derek nodded. His voice was beginning to slur. "He's definitely going to—going to look into it. When I told them we'd provide...housing, he liked that."

"What's *this* letter?" Lila shook another sheet of paper from the envelope. It was in Sinhala and handwritten; the letterhead was the monastery's: a raised bell-shaped *dagoba*. "It just says 'Please proceed as planned, with our blessings,'" Lila said. "It's from the abbot."

Derek nodded, his eyes half-closed. "Good, isn't it? Now we can make plans."

"This is for a demon ceremony?" Richard leaned forward on the couch. "What's the abbot's letter doing in the Assistant Minister's envelope?"

"Well…." Derek was leaning sideways against Sue. "They're friends, you see."

"Strange bedfellows," Richard said quietly.

Lila suddenly thought of something important. "Does this mean Zalie can come out?"

Derek's eyelids quivered. "Quite soon, dear. It's essential that—" He searched for words. Lila had never seen the furrows in his forehead so deep. "We need to be sure…where she is until the, the night of the ceremony. Then—if all goes well…"

"Of course it will." Sue smoothed his hair.

"The cat, so to speak—" Derek's lips turned up at the corners— "will be out of the bag."

This made Lila want to hug him and her mother both, so she did, half-kneeling on both their laps, her arms around their necks. Richard was standing by himself, now, looking sideways at the letters on the table. When Lila reached out and grabbed his hand, he squeezed back, almost smiling.

*

On the evening of the ceremony, Lila ran all the way from the house to the zoo area, skidding to a halt in front of Zalie's cage. The cat mewed rhythmically, staring up through the wires. Thomas the tortoise was asleep, his head and feet tucked inside his ancient shell.

"You're free!" Lila yanked the peg from the lock of the cat's cage. She threw the peg high in the air.

Zalie took a leap past Lila's open arms and ran off into the long grass. Then she scampered part way up a tree, leapt down and vanished into a thicket of weeds.

"Wait—you have to go to the ceremony!" Lila rushed after it. "Papa says so!"

A flash of orange—the cat slunk out, belly to the ground, and sprang forward. As if knowing all along that she was to go with Lila, she padded up to her and licked her ankle. Lila scooped up Zalie in her arms and strolled along the path. For a moment, things seemed just as they had always been: the crickets buzzed, the heat rose with the scent of grass, the sky grew darker purple, turning the tree branches to jagged silhouettes. Lila recalled how she'd loved murmuring secret questions to Zalie and making up the answers as she walked: *Do you think Sister Maria cheated me out of five marks on the history test? So do I. She's mean. Are Bila's shoes prettier than mine? Well they're shinier. But too round in front, like a pair of pink frogs, don't you think? I do, too!* The old cat lay with her face resting on Lila's arm. New, more complicated questions swooped at Lila—she pictured bats with sharp little fangs—yet she didn't whisper any of them to Zalie. Why not? Was she too old to talk to a cat?

It was a night of thudding drums, blazing torches, and puffs of red smoke rising in the darkness like exhalations from the mouths of invisible flame-swallowers. Lila stayed close to Richard, ostensibly so that she could explain things to him, but also because the dancers in their painted masks made her a little nervous. Sue went by with a tray of sweets and glasses of water. She looked pretty in a new skirt she'd made from a maroon batik cloth and a loose cotton top. Lila, wearing her best blue dress (though it was getting tight on her), helped her mother and Richard pass plates of food. Sue had been cooking for days but the snacks were vanishing in minutes. The flares and smoke made the night hotter, and everyone was glistening with sweat. Most of the workers on the plantation had come, along with some neighbors from nearby plantations and even some monks and shopkeepers from the crossroads.

"Do you see that mechanic we talked to last week?" Richard asked.

Lila glanced over at the tarpaulin-covered Land Rover, then searched the crowd for a man in a turban, but he wasn't here. "Not yet," she said. She did catch sight of a car in the *CAR PARK* area, whose sign had been repainted, and was relieved to see that it wasn't Hans's Jeep.

As she carried Zalie in her arms, she felt the cat's muscles tighten whenever she passed the masked dancers. Zalie hissed if one of them approached, and the dancer would back off, laughing. Lila could smell the sweat and the toddy-breath of the men; currents of energy rolled off them as they reeled past.

She and Richard moved through the crowd to the front steps to help Sue make Derek comfortable in a wicker chair that faced the front yard like an old throne. Derek was dressed in cool light slacks and shirt, but his face looked hot, beaded with sweat, his eyes red-veined and watery. Amid all the noise, he tried to explain something in his normal deep voice. Suddenly the voice swerved upwards into a high-pitched, scratchy cackle. Richard stepped back. Sue took his arm.

"Don't freak out, little brother," she whispered.

"Oh, not me!" Richard rolled his eyes.

Derek—or whoever was in him—began cursing in the strange new voice. Lila had often heard it in another part of the house; when she'd gone there to investigate, she'd found the place empty but still retaining a presence like a whiff of cigarette smoke someone's left behind in the air just after leaving a room.

"Those damned new people are spoiling my property! They let strangers come!" the voice ranted, growing squeakier. Several men and women crowded close, listening. "Everything is changed around—tables, beds, chairs! Filthy bastards, polluting my nice rooms!"

"That's old Meluwa," Lila whispered to Richard. "She's the widow who used to live in our house. She didn't want to move when her family sold it to Papa's father."

"So her spirit stayed around?" Richard said, cocking his head.

"I've heard her grumbling before," Sue said.

"You have?" Richard gave her a sideways look.

"Oh, yes." Sue laughed. Lila squinted through the tangle of hair that nearly covered Sue's eyes. On an ordinary night, her mother never would have told Richard such things. "The old lady's had too much toddy," Sue added, and then repeated it in Sinhala. Sue had had several glasses herself. People nearby laughed and nodded.

"Who's had too much?" Derek asked, his voice deep again.

"He doesn't really know when spirits get into him," Sue told Richard in a low voice.

"Evidently the place is thick with them." Richard turned to look around.

"All shapes and sizes, from mischievous to truly monstrous," Sue said.

"But they're going to get caught," Lila said.

She'd never have spoken about such things ordinarily, either, but nothing was ordinary tonight—or, she suspected, would ever be again. She pointed at two men in huge painted masks who were moving with rolling gaits toward Derek. One wore khaki shorts, and undershirt, and a purple wooden face with bulging spiral eyes; his head sprouted waves of thick blond straw that rustled as he rocked from side to side. The other man had on a gauzy pink dress below his mask. His wooden face was more fearsome than the first man's, with huge hairy eyebrows arched above eye holes and tusks protruded from the grinning mouth. Beside them a drummer danced in place, pounding out a deep, thudding rhythm.

Men and women crowded close, waiting, their faces shiny from the reflections of the flames. Part of Lila's mind coolly memorized the dancers' colors and expressions and positions for future paintings, another part was in the night with them, amazed, delighted, frightened all at once and glad to be near Mum and Richard. Her father, his eyes closed, seemed to be elsewhere, though he was sitting right there.

"First you have to attract the demons—by making them think you're one of them and you have presents for them," Lila heard Sue say to Richard, explaining why the dancers looked so ferocious. "Then you have to catch the demons in those things." She pointed out the covered baskets that had been placed around the yard.

"But can you keep all the demons in them?" Richard asked. To Lila, he looked really foreign in his jeans and checked shirt and broad-brimmed hat—but then, it too appeared to be a kind of costume, as strange to the people here as the masks were to him, probably.

"Keep them all in the baskets?" Sue frowned. "I suppose it depends on how much you believe. I'm just trying to explain things, Richard."

"Okay. How *long* can you keep the demons shut up?"

"I don't know!" Sue turned away. "Leave me alone, will you?"

Suddenly he gripped her arm. "Who the hell's *that?*"

Lila saw him point to a tall man dressed in red robes, his face painted red. His head was bristling with flame-colored straw hair. In his hand was a rope with which he was slashing a tusked black-masked demon.

"That's Katagarama. One of the strong gods, all red like Mars. Derek's been waiting for him," Sue said. "He's one of the good guys, so don't worry."

"But the one with the tusks—he's a demon, right?"

"A bad one." Sue nodded. The demon was hugging a light-colored plastic doll to his chest.

"I've seen that guy before," Richard said to Lila.

"Me, too." Lila frowned. He looked just like the monster in the temple painting who'd been kidnapping a screaming white woman. This demon had already bitten off the doll's plastic arm. Now he spread her legs and began thrusting his pelvis between them. The crowd laughed uneasily. The monster gasped and groaned, going into a frenzy of leg-movements like a dancer in a music video. Soot-speckled smoke drifted over him. Then the tall red god-figure smacked him across the face with the rope. He howled, and the doll rolled free onto the grass. The demon did a cartwheel and landed in some thorns. A roar went up from the crowd.

"Stay away from this plantation, monster!"

"Die, stinking Tamil child-fucker!" someone shouted.

Lila didn't translate the curses for Richard. He was looking confused enough as it was, his own face shiny with sweat, his hat slipped at an angle on his head. She felt the cat squirming in her arms, and sat on the steps below her father's chair.

"Let Zalie reveal herself!" A high scratchy voice exhorted her. Derek leaned forward, his eyes rolled back so that the whites shone in the flickery light. "Let her walk!"

Lila released the cat. Several men and women stepped back, watching Zalie pad across the grass. The tall red god followed her carefully, muttering in Sinhala.

"Evidently," Sue said, "the god thinks a demon may have possessed the cat weeks ago, as a way of getting into the plantation."

"Like a kind of scout?" Richard asked.

"Yes."

"Is that why Papa kept her penned up?" Lila leaned close to her mother to be heard over the drumming.

"Probably," Sue said.

The cat stopped and lay still in the grass. Gradually people stopped watching her, but no one left the area.

"This is one hell of a party," Richard said to Lila. "Have you ever seen anything like it?"

Lila shook her head. All the people running back and forth, the smell of incense, smoke and food, the snatches of song—it was fun, exciting drama; it made her want to run and do cartwheels like the demon dancers. But for a brief moment she sensed something evil was getting into the ceremony, was stinking around the edge of the smoke, was singeing the flame-lit figures; it was trying to take over the ceremony while the people were trying to keep it away.

And where was Zalie now? In a corner of the yard Lila saw a wall of woven palm-fronds that someone had put up—a place to catch demons. On a platform before the screen was a big woven basket. That was where Zalie had scampered off to. Now she nosed around the basket. Everyone went silent, standing back. Lila covered her eyes.

She felt Richard's hand on her shoulder and peeked out between her fingers. "If Zalie goes in the basket…"

And then Zalie did. The people gave out a gasp, which quickly turned to confused murmuring. A second went by. Then the cat jumped out again. The red-haired god snatched Zalie up from the ground and handed her to Lila. The cat looked up at her, pointed teeth vanishing into soft furry mouth.

"Well, that's good," Sue said, letting out her breath.

Richard nodded. "Zalie proved her innocence, right? Or not?"

"*I* think so," Lila said, and pushed her face into the cat's fur. "You did, didn't you?" she whispered to Zalie. The cat purred.

After midnight, the power of the demons seemed to be in decline, yet the god Katagarama still hadn't approached Derek. Exorcist-dancers tormented demons with loud jokes. One dancer accused a demon-figure of shitting on the beach like a drunken tourist. The crowd roared with laughter. Dancers swirled, their bright shirts fanning out; they leapt over fires and shouted triumphantly. Among the smells of spicy food wove the potent scent of *bhang;* Lila inhaled long breaths of the smoke from a man's fat cigarette, its perfume spreading deliciously up her nostrils. She sat on the steps between her mother and Richard now, dozing and waking, hearing snatches of songs, chants and mantras.

Once she heard a scratchy voice from close by—from her father's mouth, in fact. "An intruder is weakening us! An intruder—has to go back—has to leave us alone—"

But people crowded around to yell back to the spirit—"No! Where is your hospitality? Don't shame us!"

The man in red slapped a basket upside down next to Derek's feet. "Got the rotten little rubbish-mouth!" he shouted, and gave the basket a kick down the stairs. Everyone laughed as it rolled off into the bushes.

Derek opened his eyes slowly. "Where's the *arak?*" he asked, the voice deep and funny and his own again. "I want to give some to Katagarama!"

The watchman shuffled up with an old gin bottle half full of yellow liquid. A glass was poured; the tall god took a long drink and raised his eyes to the sky as people cheered. Sue took a drink, then Derek drank until he choked. Richard held the glass for a moment, then passed it on. Lila settled down on the step close to her mother, half-closing her eyes.

The yard whirled in the cooling air, flames blowing sideways, spicy smells rushing past her nose. The overhanging tree leaves changed slowly from black to green as the bonfires' flames rose and fell. She pictured a girl like her galloping round and round the yard on the back of a white horse, her cheek resting against its soft white mane. When she opened her eyes again, Katagarama was dancing in front of her father.

"Mum?" Lila reached up to tug her mother's hand.

"Shhh, watch," Sue said. "Finally...."

The god stood over Derek, moving some snarled pieces of vine along his hair. Behind the god, just visible in the darkness, monks in saffron robes watched and murmured. Someone had tied vines around Derek's head, the knots tight on his forehead, leaves falling over his eyes. The god hummed mantras as he touched the vines. Lila could see sweat beading in the red dye on his cheeks, blurring the kohl around his bloodshot eyes. Each vine seemed to unravel beneath the god's arched fingers. Finally he swept all the vines away. They tumbled down the steps. Derek's head rose, his mouth opening.

The god stepped back, filling the air with a mantra that called on all spirits and *devas* to untie the knotted veins under the skin of Derek's forehead, to unsnarl all the tangles of his worries, and set his mind at peace. "Let him take refuge in the *sangha*, the community of all who revere the Buddha and his teachings," Katagarama intoned.

Lila felt her own lips moving with the god's prayer. Sue, too, was speaking silently, her eyes shut. Only Richard was still standing back, watching.

"*The jewel is in the blossom of the lotus....*" Lila whispered, and pictured herself reflected in a drop of dew that lay quivering among the silky petals of a flower.

Her father stood up, his hands covering his forehead. Slowly he let them fall. His eyes blinked open. The tight lines in his forehead were gone. "No more pain," he said, his mouth staying open as he exhaled. "It's *gone!*"

Sue reached up and grabbed his hand. Her cheeks were damp, and so were Lila's as she wrapped her arms around her father's waist.

People began to wander away. The red god left. Lila sat down on the top step while her father, looking drained but still smiling, dropped back into his wicker chair. The dawn light flowed through the trees, a silver glow scented like the coals that still smoked in braziers around the yard. Zalie lay on the warm stone beside Lila. Everyone was here but Richard.

Lila saw him at the top of the driveway, gazing down the hill. Several saffron-robed figures descended past him and vanished behind some bushes. In a few moments she heard the faint rumble of their car starting. Soon the noise faded, leaving behind the lovely dawn sounds Lila had woken to every morning of her life: the pulse of insects, the chatter and squawk of birds. Richard, standing still in the grass, seemed to be listening to them, too.

Lila rested her cheek on her mother's soft skirt. Smiling, she shut her eyes and slept.

TEN

Years later, when Lila painted pictures of life at its best on the plantation, she remembered the radiant week just after the ceremony, the last days before the arrival of demons that no one could exorcise.

During that time, her father stepped out of his dungeon of pain and embraced his family again. Lila heard the deep rumble of his laugh that she'd always loved. He called her *pol* again. Practically every time he saw her he gave her a quick hug, his beard brushing her forehead—as if he'd just come back from a long journey. He hugged Sue, too, in ways that both embarrassed and delighted Lila. Sue, flustered at first, became more animated every day. As she worked, she rediscovered the extraordinary pleasure you could get from pulling a carrot out of the soil or smelling a freshly laundered towel on a clothesline. Lila was as happy as she'd been before Richard arrived. No, happier: now both Richard and her father were eager to look at the pictures in her portfolio, to read books to her and be read to, to play cards and go for endless walks.

By an unspoken agreement, the family talked only of the plantation and the sanctuary—which were now officially the same place. Again Derek spoke of animals he would bring here to thrive amid the lush vegetation, to roam freely in spacious enclosed habitats where visitors could appreciate their beauty without harming them or their environment. Perhaps an elephant could be a kind of greeter at the front gate, with someone riding its neck wearing a spangly golden turban and gown.

"Do we know someone the right age—a girl almost twelve, say, with golden skin and blue eyes?" Derek asked.

"Yes!" Lila screamed. "Yes!"

A pair of giraffes would certainly be a big attraction. Derek showed everyone a newspaper clipping about an international wildlife organization that was looking for homes for animals endangered by wars in Africa. With government help, many creatures might come here. He and Lila, Sue and Richard, poured over illustrations of animals in big zoology texts that hadn't been off the shelves since Lila had been a small child. Never mind that worms had bored tiny tunnels though the pages; worms were part of nature, too, and paper had become their environment.

Of course the country was rich in its own fauna; when the workers (soon to be on the government payroll) cleared paths through jungle areas, who could tell what sorts of mammals, reptiles, birds might be discovered? And flora—the place was already an enormous garden, some of it domestic and labeled, much of it still wild and best left so—teeming with undisturbed beneficent spirits, Derek laughed. New books on managing nature parks must be available in America, Derek said. Richard said he and his fiancée had read some at the local college library for their courses. Derek said he'd order copies right away.

Here—they were sitting at the dinner table, finishing a dish of fresh mangoes—Derek looked at Sue and asked, "Who would manage the business part of the sanctuary? The ministry will provide a good salary."

"Not me," Sue said, "I've got this house, and you know how you are with numbers...."

Lila's hand pumped in the air as if she were at her classroom desk. "Richard and Raquel!"

Derek leaned back in his chair and smiled at Richard—for the first time in a long time—and asked, "Would you consider it?"

"Yes! Why not? Yes!" Lila tugged Richard's arm.

"It's something to think about," he said. "I'll write Raquel."

"Brilliant! Smashing!" Lila said, using her schoolgirl words. Now her last worry—that Richard would go back to America for good—vanished. All the family would stay together—and with a new auntie. Lila carried Raquel's postcard with her everywhere as a talisman, and began a series of pastels to mail to her, to entice her to come.

School—a week away—seemed a less odious prospect; she'd have so many things to tell Radha now. She finished all her holiday assignments so as to spend time helping to do a "survey" of the sanctuary. In fact, she was "project cartographer": she drew maps showing where gardens and pools and picnic areas would be, as Derek, talking all the while with Richard, pointed out patches of grass or brambles or jungle. Richard looked over Lila's work, grinning at the animals and plants that decorated each area. If Richard minded that Derek had discussed many of the same plans with him two years before, he didn't show it.

When Lila, Derek, and Richard walked along the plantation's outer fence, Derek repaired the breaks he found in the barbed wire (surprisingly, there were still a lot of them) but was no longer obsessed with walking over the same areas checking that every last bamboo post was in place. Guards hadn't been sent by the Ministry yet (this surprised him, too), but at the gates no gangs of boys lurked about waiting for a chance to snatch fruit or make menacing remarks. In fact, people on the road hurried past now, most keeping their eyes straight ahead. Perhaps they'd been awed by the visit of the high government official, Richard suggested.

"Perhaps. And the ceremony we gave—it helped us regain our social position in the area," Derek explained to Richard as they walked along one of the shaggy paths. "Now and then, you have to show you're strong enough to sort of cleanse the neighborhood."

"Of dangerous spirits?" Richard asked, cocking his head.

"Well, people believe that." Derek smiled.

"My fiancée would have some ideas." Richard chewed a piece of twig as he walked along. "She's a believer. When I told her about being here two years ago, she said, 'There's got to be some kind of powerful energy there that helped you.' And in a way, I believe that."

Derek ruffled Lila's hair. "It's possible. Look how much better I feel. How can we explain it?"

"I've been thinking about that ceremony." Richard paused in the red-tinted shade of a poinciana tree. "It seems to me that it has to help a person when a huge number of family and friends and neighbors go to a lot of trouble putting on dramatic rituals in his honor. They cheer and celebrate, and they show their belief in their power over evil."

"So—it's a kind of emotional contagion," Derek said.

"Sure. More than that, too. If the person has any belief of his own, even if the belief's just in his memory, and if he knows that everyone expects him to believe and improve…"

Derek said, "He becomes part of the collective will…."

Most of these words Lila didn't understand, but she remembered them; she liked storing away words as well as images. What she liked best was just walking along with her father and Richard, being included in the talk, and looking at the sanctuary again as she had before her father had become sick. Flowers bloomed from bushes, coconuts fell crashing into the underbrush, mangos dangled from the tree branches—all to be sniffed, picked, gathered.

When her father and mother were busy, Lila wandered around the paths with Richard. Once, near the jungle boundary, she stopped short, crying out as something solid and alive leapt across the path ahead of her. It was brown, heavy, with wild eyes. Its hooves seemed to flick along the ground, it landed so lightly as it ran. Then it vanished with a crash into the underbrush. She heard it galloping off; the sound didn't fade, it just stopped, as if the creature had jumped into midair and never come down.

Richard stared after it. "A *sambhur*, right? The animal you hear but never see?"

"But we did see it!" Lila glanced up at his face; his grin verified that the deer really had gone by right in front of them. "I was never so close to one before. I can still smell it, can you?"

"Yeah. Sort of musky." Richard took a long breath. "It was like a sleek pony."

"That's a kind of horse," Lila said, almost to herself. She was picturing the deer—too young to have horns, a flash of golden light amid the foliage but substantial enough for her to remember and sketch endlessly afterwards.

Sometimes Richard wanted to sit down, looking out over the land, and write in his journal. Lila sketched him with her pastel pencils. Sitting on the high slope among the rubber trees, she watched the sun sparkling on the paddy fields below—a series of rectangular ponds whose borders seemed to blur in the distance. Lila drew them as if they were being filled by blue sky poured into molds down the sides of the faraway hills. And meanwhile Richard wrote— perhaps about the same scene she was sketching. Or perhaps he was writing about her drawing him, while she drew him writing. She liked that idea, picturing two mirrors stuck upright in the earth.

Once Richard said, "I'm writing as fast as I can these days. At first I recorded things so I'd have them to mail to Raquel. Now they seem to be for me."

On her pad, Lila shaded in some dark lines around Richard's eyes. The skin there wrinkled as he looked around. He didn't look upset, as he had two years ago, just wary, waiting.

"Do you write down only what you see?" she asked.

"Other things, too. Sometimes I don't know what my thoughts are until I write them."

Lila looked at her drawing. "I know what you mean."

"Not that it's helped me figure out what to do, so far." Richard closed his journal, a cardboard-bound book with metal rings along the spine.

They walked to the zoo. Lila pulled up some leaves that Thomas the tortoise liked. The cat, Zalie, never went near her old cage, and often disappeared for hours at a time these days, but Thomas was always where she'd left him. His cage door was still shut so he couldn't wander off and get stolen and be sold to tourists. Inside he had a little watering hole that the rains filled for him every evening. And all meals provided by the management, as Derek liked to say. When Lila squatted down to poke the greens in at him, his face slowly appeared from under his mottled gold and black shell.

"He's got such huge sad eyes, when he opens them all the way," Lila said. "I wonder if he'd rather be free."

"Probably." Richard squatted beside her.

"His shell's beautiful." Lila reached in to touch it. The ridges were sharp, its little valleys smooth, and the edges scalloped. "He's never seen himself, probably. So he doesn't know he's beautiful."

"You could paint his picture."

"Right! And show it to him." Lila stood up. "Next time I come out here, I'll bring my paints."

But she forgot—the next time, and the time after that. And then years went by before she would paint a picture of the tortoise, from memory.

*

Cricket/softball games were more lively with Derek playing again. He slow-bowled Lila with easy bounces that allowed her to whack the tennis ball against the house and off the trees. She ran shrieking around the pitch, jumping with both feet onto one of the safe "bases" seconds before the ball was clanged against the wicket. Card games went on later and later at night, as if no one ever wanted to stop playing, as tired as they were. Power cuts were more frequent; without the fan blades whirring, Lila sweated onto her cards and wiped her eyes with damp cloths. Derek now played poker, even bluffing occasionally. Match piles grew higher around the table; Lila won over a thousand wooden rupees by the end of the week.

It was on a Sunday, eight days after the ceremony, when Sue brought some strange news to report at dinner. Lila would always recall that evening because it was the first night that Zalie wasn't curled up on her bed in the next room; Lila didn't know where she was.

"Do you remember during the ceremony when the *preta* said we had an intruder who'd come to hurt us?" Sue asked, turning to Derek. He nodded.

"I thought I was the intruder," Richard said.

"Of course you aren't," Sue said. "You're family."

"I know I'd been getting on your nerves sometimes." Richard turned to Derek.

"Not at all." Derek put down his fork. "Everything was getting me down then. Anyway, I'm not sure who it was that mentioned an intruder—I don't remember it at all."

"You really don't?" Richard asked.

Derek glanced at him over the water pitcher. Lila noticed that Richard was wearing his *Cheyenne Frontier Days* T-shirt; his hair was pulled back and fastened behind, and his chin was dark with stubble. As she saw him through her father's eyes for a moment, he suddenly looked more out-of-place here than usual.

"I truly don't remember." Derek picked up his fork again.

Sue leaned forward, her glasses shifting crooked on her face. "I think there *is* an intruder around here—not on the plantation, but nearby. And I think it's Hans."

"You've never liked him," Derek said.

"True. But listen, Derek, Daya told me that Hans is in deep trouble. As tolerant as people are here—well, he's crossed the line."

Now Derek, Richard, and Lila were quiet, watching Sue. According to Daya, whose ear was always to the ground, Hans had, as usual, invited several toddy-tappers to his hotel to drink with him last week. They were disreputable people, Sue said, disliked by local farmers and plantation workers. As the night's party got louder, Hans had accused one of the tappers of stealing his money. This was a brother of Hans's woman, Meenu, who was now very swollen with the expected baby. "When she tried to make peace between Hans and her brother, Hans smacked her across the face with the back of his hand and knocked her to the floor." Sue paused. "I never knew why you put up with that crazy bastard," she said to Derek.

Derek shook his head slowly.

"What happened then?" Lila asked, leaning over her plate.

"Meenu's brother took her away with him," Sue said. "And the men who worked for Hans left, too—every last one of them. He's all alone in that hotel."

"Nothing happened to Hans?" Richard asked.

"Nothing yet," Sue said.

"He can't run that big place by himself," Derek said. "I'll have to check on him."

"That's a terrible idea." Sue bit her lip. She didn't take her eyes off Derek.

"He's very vulnerable out there," Derek said, frowning. "Those tappers are violent people. They'll do anything—"

"Hans was the one who was violent." Sue sat back in her chair. "You've said yourself he was taking too many risks."

Derek picked up his water glass and took a sip. It might have contained clear vinegar, Lila thought, the way his forehead suddenly wrinkled and his eyes went damp. "Listen, I'm doing everything in my power to protect us here," he said, his voice booming. The water glass clunked down to the table in his fist. "If I have to see that Hans is all right, I have to. You don't know everything that's going on—"

"If I don't, it's because you haven't told me." Sue wiped her face with her napkin. "Things have been so good recently. Why do we have to risk helping someone who nobody around here can stand?"

Richard had been turning his head back and forth. Now he looked straight at Derek. "Can you tell us why we have to do anything for Hans?" he asked.

"How could you understand?" Derek stood up from the table, his chair scraping against the floor. "You don't live here."

"You don't have to be here very long to see what Hans is like." Sue pushed her glasses up her nose, taking a long look at Derek.

He pressed his fingertips hard against his forehead, his face turned sideways.

"I've got some ideas about Hans now, Sue," Richard said. He stared down at the tablecloth. "Hans is very rich, but he's still put himself at risk around here with his crazy behavior."

"Not for the first time," Sue said.

"Right." Richard kept his voice even. "Anyway, Hans comes to our place to talk business one day. Soon afterwards, a dumb, neutral foreigner—me—is given a packet of something to take to the abbot at the monastery. Let's suppose it's money in the packet—German Deutchmarks. And the abbot, who's the main power guy around here, takes his cut, and then he delivers the rest to the Assistant Minister for Ecological Affairs."

"That's nonsense!" Derek slammed the table with the flat of his hand. "How can you talk like that in my house?"

"I haven't finished." Richard narrowed his eyes. "This Assistant Minister, he's an official who could never personally do business with a wild-ass guy like Hans. Any more than the Buddhist holy roller could. But the deal gets done in this roundabout way, and suddenly we're designated a government-protected park."

Sue stared at Richard, then up at Derek. "Is any of this true?" she asked.

"I told you, I am doing everything I can to protect us," Derek said.

"But if Hans has just been deserted by his whole entourage and lost his woman—what does that mean for us?" Richard asked.

"I don't know," Sue said.

"I don't know, either," Richard said. "But I don't think it'd be good for us if Hans gets even stranger and starts talking too much. That must have occurred to you, Derek."

Derek nodded slowly. Sue stared at him.

"What's Hans *doing?*" Lila asked, filling the silence.

Sue rested her hand on Lila's arm, then turned back to Derek. "Listen to me—do you know what Daya told me Hans is up to?" Her voice dropped; Lila leaned closer to hear. "All day," Sue continued, "Hans wanders around that shooting range of his, smoking heroin and blasting away at clay targets with a pistol."

"Damn it," Derek whispered.

Silence rushed into the room and took up all the space. Lila pictured it as sooty smoke.

"Hans...." Richard shook his head. "How alone can anyone be?" Lila watched his fingertips dig into the tablecloth. "It couldn't get any worse than that," he said.

ELEVEN

Putting on her school uniform—Lila would believe years later—must have seemed like a magical way of keeping herself the same girl she'd been before the holidays. As she stared into the long mirror beside her bureau, she saw a child in child's clothes—the familiar knee socks, green skirt, white blouse, and loose green necktie. Yet she had missed a lot in that framed glass rectangle. When the mirror image appeared years later in a self-portrait done from memory, her lips had begun to develop a tightness they would never lose, and the eyelids had already developed a faint downward slope at their outer corners. On the canvas, the play of light in her eyes looked like the reflection of a faraway fire.

That morning, Lila put out of her mind Richard's argument with her father last night at dinner and accepted what her mother had told her—that Richard wasn't upset anymore, and that her father's headache was temporary. Now she kept her mind busy with school thoughts, especially the news she would whisper to Radha in chapel about Richard and Raquel coming here. In her knapsack, along with her books and sketchpad, Lila slipped the postcard of Sakajawea. She wondered if she ought to go look for Zalie, who was missing again, but there wasn't time.

That Monday, everyone in the family tried hard to help her believe that life was the same as always. Her mother ironed her uniform; it was still warm when she put it on and had a lovely baked scent to it. Her father, coming out of the bedroom in his crisp slacks and bush shirt, quizzed her on the material for a history test she'd been studying for.

And to show there were no hard feelings, he asked Richard if he'd wait with Lila for the bullock bus at the gate.

"Occasionally the driver's sleeping off a night of toddy-tippling," Derek said, "and he doesn't show up on time."

"Sometimes not at all," Sue said, smiling.

And so Lila and Richard walked to the gate, both carrying umbrellas; the clouds were low and gray above the treetops. Soon they burst, sending Lila and Richard running down the driveway. Ruts in the surface became rivulets and turned to little rushing brooks by the time Lila reached the main gate and took shelter under the platform. On the gate's other side, raindrops blown slantways panged against the metal as if desperately trying to get in.

Daya opened the gate a crack so they could watch for the bullock bus, but it was hard to see more than a few yards out into the road. Some flat-bed trucks loaded with cane rumbled by; it was the cane-harvest season now. Daya complained that several people had taken advantage of the weather to climb over the other plantation gates, thinking that no one would be patrolling in the rain. They'd ignored his shouts and headed for one of the half-collapsed outbuildings, carrying long canvas-wrapped bundles. Daya had phoned the house, but the phone's batteries there must have been down, because no one had picked up.

"Oops," Lila said. She'd taken on the job of charging the phones, but last night she had so much on her mind that she'd forgotten. Richard said he'd do it when he went back to the house, and he would take Daya's message.

As they waited, Daya told them more news about Hans: his woman, Meenu, had run away from her brothers and gone back to him at the hotel. Lila was glad when Daya climbed back to his observation post; she didn't want to talk about Hans anymore. She liked watching the road's surface, with its patterns of noisily splashing raindrops creating a mist. The paddy fields on the other side seemed to be boiling and bubbling as the rain struck the standing water. Then something appeared crawling slowly across the road like a green ghost. It was only a monitor lizard, walking with a slow precise gait, oblivious to the weather, its legs bent, its narrow black tongue flicking in and out. Lila pictured the tongue as a little snake trying repeatedly to escape the long green mouth.

"Those guys still look fantastic to me," Richard said, standing behind her.

"You once said they looked like a cross between a crocodile and a dinosaur," Lila said.

"Well, they do." Richard smiled. "But you grew up around them. If you were at my place and saw a woodchuck coming out of its hole, you'd probably be amazed, too."

Lila had no idea what a woodchuck could be—perhaps a big reptile that ate wood. But she didn't ask, because she was repeating the words "if you were at my place" in her head and half-hoping, half-dreading that Richard would ask her again to visit him. She didn't know then what she would say, and just watched the lizard. It stopped, then quickly turned its snout and scrambled off into the underbrush—the way Zalie sometimes did when strangers approached. Now two workers from the next plantation hurried along the road, holding pieces of thick transparent plastic over their heads. They shouted up to Daya that the school's bullock-bus driver wasn't coming today; his cart had broken down.

When this had happened before, Daya had taken Lila on the luggage carrier of his bicycle. Richard said he would do it today; he wanted to look for the mechanic at the crossroads, anyway. They waited until the rain stopped, as it always did in the mornings; in a few minutes sunlight was glittering in the raindrops left on leaves and flower petals. Puddles glowed on the road, and green hills reappeared so bright they looked illuminated from the inside. Daya wrapped a dry cloth around the metal carrier on the bicycle's rear fender, and Lila sat sideways on it as he held the cycle steady.

Richard wasn't used to riding with a passenger behind him, and had trouble pedaling in a straight line at first. Lila whooped, laughing, as the bicycle tilted and once nearly swerved into an irrigation ditch. Men and women stepped out of their little houses to watch the foreigner zigzag along. She waved at them. The road was coming to life again after the rain, filling with people riding bicycles and motor scooters, walking and leading buffaloes by long ropes. Another truck full of cane roared by, the workers sitting in back with their machetes, calling out to pretty women who turned their faces away and giggled.

Lila liked the downhill slopes, when the bicycle coasted, just swooping along the line of the road. But on one long hill, the road veered off to the right at a V, and Richard coasted with it off the main road. By the time they reached the bottom, it was too late to make a sharp reverse turn. Still, this road would rejoin the main one after a mile or so. Lila raised her head to say this in Richard's ear.

"I'll just keep going then," he said.

"Right." As soon as she said it, she wished she hadn't—this road went past Hans's hotel.

The long high wall came into view, sunlight flickering off the stones set in the cement. The bicycle tire slipped in a patch of mud; both Richard and Lila had to poke their feet out to keep from toppling. That was when they heard the scream from behind the wall.

It was the most dreadful sound Lila had ever heard—high-pitched, jagged, a cry of frenzied disbelief and horror. On it went like a streak of red slashing back and forth through the air. *"Nein!—no!—nein!"* The open-throated shriek turned to loud, terrible sobs.

Richard skidded to a halt, reaching one arm back to hold Lila upright. He let the bicycle fall beneath him with a clatter. Lila's knapsack flopped off one shoulder as she stumbled and stood up. She heard a loud crack; afterwards she would remember it like a huge piece of glass being broken just overhead. A flash of silence followed the noise; she grabbed Richard's arm tight. Then came the sound of someone running.

Out past the open gate a man in a filthy sarong appeared. He turned his face, and Lila saw the small dark eyes, the lips parted in a grin, the flicker of white teeth, the matted black hair. The man ran off into the underbrush, the branches crackling around him. Richard pulled Lila back down the road, but she couldn't stop watching the gate.

Hans staggered into the road. In one hand he waved a pistol in the air. *Click, click, click!* it went. His other hand covered his face. From behind it, the screaming sobs began again.

Lila pushed her cheek hard against Richard's arm. Hans's pistol dropped to the road. Both of his hands rose to his face, now, fingers bent as if he were trying to claw off a layer of skin. Above his fingertips his yellow hair bristled in the sunlight. Wearing only tight shorts, he seemed horribly naked against the dark wall. He staggered in place like a mad puppet with tangled strings. His knees wobbled, the pale legs gave way beneath him, and now he was rolling over and over in the road, still sobbing, the cries no longer muffled by his hands. Finally Lila saw his face. One side of it was the color and texture of freshly butchered market beef. The nose was a raw red lump. His eyes were wet, one of them a scalded-out hollow. Sprawled on his side, he curled into a tight, whimpering ball.

Another man rushed out of the gate with a long-handled metal pot in his hand. He flung it at Hans. It missed him and came rolling against the fallen bicycle's crossbar with a clang.

"Don't touch it!" Richard shouted.

"What is it?" Lila froze, staring at the pot.

"I think it's acid."

She heard footsteps, then another voice—a girl crying out. Meenu, wild-haired and round-bellied in a faded blue housedress, rushed into the road.

"Hans!" Meenu fell to her knees beside him, one hand grasping at the top of his spiky head. She turned her face up to Richard. *"Help us!"* she screamed.

Then Lila became a frantic translator, shouting messages back and forth between Richard and Meenu. "Have you got a telephone inside?"—"Yes, but I don't know how it works!"—"You push the number buttons!"—"What numbers do I push?"—"I don't know, is there a book, a directory?"—"I can't read books, please, please get us a doctor!" And all the while, Hans rolled on the ground, his hands pressed to his face.

"I could use their phone," Lila whispered to Richard.

"We're not going in there!" he told her.

Then she heard a rumbling sound—an old flat-bed truck was winding down the road toward them. "Look!" Lila pointed.

Richard moved to the middle of the road, standing with both arms high in the air, blocking the truck's way. Its brakes screeched, and it stopped several yards from Hans.

One of the men in the cab spoke English. At first, he didn't want to transport the crumpled-up German anywhere, but Meenu's wailings convinced him. He and the driver lifted Hans onto the back of the truck, where they set him down on some jute sacks among the cane stalks. Meenu climbed up beside him. Richard helped Lila up into the cab, then he and one of the men sat in back with Hans as the truck bumped along. Even with the roar of the engine filling the cab, Lila could hear Hans's high-pitched sobs flying into the air behind her.

To keep from trembling, she pressed her knuckles to her lips and stared hard out the open window. The cab was roasting hot and stank of diesel fuel. The closer it came to the crossroads, the fewer people Lila saw on the normally busy road, but she felt so breathless and strange she hardly paid much attention to this until she passed the little SPRITE sweetshop where she'd taken Richard. No one was sitting on the chairs in its yard. Its door and wooden shutters were shut tight.

The truck's gears scraped as it slowed to approach the crossroads. Now Lila noticed how different the houses looked today—their windows and doors were also shut. No children played in yards, no women hung out clothes on ropes strung between trees. Lila felt as if she were riding through the deepest, quietest part of the night while everyone was inside, but without the darkness keeping the huddled houses from view. The turnoff to the monastery was normally a busy intersection where saffron-robed monks and novices drank little glasses of tea at a roadside shop. No one stood beside the gravel entrance today except two uniformed soldiers, rifles held at their hips.

As soon as the truck turned into the main market square, the driver braked hard, gripping the top of the steering wheel with both hands. He let out a sudden moan. The windshield on Lila's side was so streaked with dirt that she had to lean out of the side window to see what was ahead. The market stalls, usually packed with people, were almost deserted—though all of the fruits and vegetables, boxes and crates, piles of sandals and stacks of clothes were still displayed in the open air. Here and there a man covered a stall with a tarpaulin, as if expecting a downpour, though the sky was a cloudless blue. The truck's engine stalled. Lila squinted hard at the stucco buildings before her.

She recognized one in particular, a white two-story, flat-roofed house standing beside a pile of rubble. The house had no side wall. She could see into a kitchen, a sitting room, and on the second floor, a bedroom with a bed and bureau and cupboard. She had been in all of these rooms, herself. She knew them. She knew the people who lived in them. How could she be looking into them now—with no outside wall? Where were the people?

Pushing open the cab door, she stumbled down onto the road. She realized she'd never seen the house from this part of the road before. That was because it was ordinarily behind another two-story building, the clinic…which was somehow no longer there. All that remained of it were huge chunks of concrete and plaster, wood beams and shards of glass lying all over the ground. She took a wobbly step forward and stopped, listening, as if for some explanation. But a great silence rushed at her.

She walked slowly forward, taking raspy breaths. There in the house's sitting room was the Sharmas' couch…the gold-fabric easy chair…the polished wooden coffee table. Everything was covered in soot. The door to the kitchen was ajar as if Mrs. Sharma in her sari would come walking through it at any moment carrying a birthday cake before her. There was the television in its corner, but the screen was blank. Not blank—its screen was missing; the tangled wires behind it were visible. The bride-doll's glass case was gone from its shelf. On the floor the doll lay on its back, its gauzy dress and veil and plaster skin glowing sugary white. It seemed to have floated down from the sky like a butterfly or an angel and was resting for a moment on a sparkly bed of broken glass.

Where was Radha? For a moment, Lila's eyes filled with tears as she remembered her friend in her nurse's cap—the way it looked above Radha's plump face, and how it felt when Radha had put it on Lila's head once—too big, with the brim nearly covering her eyes.

Now Lila gazed at jagged slices of glass, upended chairs, dozens of plastic bottles, unraveled bandage rolls—the clinic was exposed and lying everywhere. A long table was smashed, collapsed in the middle as if some enormous creature had stomped on its back. There had been a fire—light-colored objects were charred with black streaks, half-burnt wooden beams lay amid the rubble, and strange shapes of singed cloth drooped everywhere. As she came closer, a stench rose—smoke, disinfectant, acrid burnt mattress stuffing. She waved her hand in front of her face as if to push the smell away, but it floated over her, making her eyes sting. And still she heard nothing but the empty pulsing in the air like a scream trying to burst out of an open mouth.

Then Richard was speaking to her, and soldiers were telling him and the truck driver to leave the area. A child was crying somewhere behind a stack of towels. A white van came rumbling up. Lila heard English and Sinhala sentences all tangling together along with unintelligible grunts and gasps from Hans. He was squirming in place on the back of the truck among the cane stalks. Two policemen lifted him and pushed him headfirst into the back of a van. Meenu crawled in, too, her plump legs and behind visible beneath her tight blue dress. Hans would be taken to a hospital in Colombo, one soldier told Richard. The van drove off.

The silence was hiding now between the voices of people and the rumbles of engines and the crackles of radios from a police van and even among the notes of squealing music from a radio someone must have left on under an awning. Lila wondered if she'd ever stop hearing—feeling, sensing—this awful emptiness. She couldn't stand the silence; she filled it with her own voice.

"Where's Radha?" she asked. "Where's Dr. Sharma? Mrs. Sharma?"

"I don't know," Richard said.

"Are they hurt?"

He took her hand in his. "We'll find out, Lila."

They walked around trying to find someone who knew something, but people either had no information or were afraid to say what they knew. Walls were scorched black. Everything smelled of burnt cloth and charred wood. Glass crunched underfoot as people walked by. The windows of nearly every building were smudged or shattered. Behind one window, an old woman was moving a cloth back and forth—carefully washing the soot from the sharp half-piece of glass that remained in the frame. Several men and women were waiting around the blown-off clinic door—out of habit perhaps, or perhaps just because they'd already walked miles and miles to get here and were in pain and still needed a doctor. It was hard to believe that there wasn't a doctor somewhere, despite all the rubble. At first it made Lila mad, seeing these waiting people—you blow up the Sharmas' place and then you want them to be here!—but when she came closer and saw the people's faces—they looked confused, sick, half-crazed with worry—her anger at them dissolved in the smoky air.

She and Richard found themselves at the school. Sheltered behind some other buildings, it hadn't been damaged but its front door was locked, its yard empty. Lila pressed her face to the window but saw only empty desks and chairs and freshly scrubbed blackboards. She looked around the area for girls in uniforms, but saw no one. Then she spotted a man with a round knitted cap—the Moslem taxi-man Richard had spoken to when he was last here. Richard caught up with him and asked what had happened.

"I don't know much." The man shook his head slowly, his eyes big and sad. "What I heard was, early this morning—it was before many customers came to the market—a big bomb blew up the clinic. People said the Tamil Tigers did the thing because the Tamil doctor and his wife were government civil servants—'collaborators.'" The man sighed. "Their crime was that they treated everyone— Sinhalese, Tamil—alike."

"Their crime...." Richard stared at the ground.

"What about the house behind the clinic?" Lila cried. "What about the Sharmas? Are they all right?"

"I'm sorry, I don't know." The man spoke softly. "But people say the clinic was not open when the bomb went off."

"What *happened* to them?" Lila shrieked. *"Where are they? Where's Radha?"*

The taxi driver looked at Richard, then past him at the rubble. All he'd heard was that some ambulance vans had driven down the road toward Colombo full of wounded people. No one seemed to know who they were. One person was killed for sure: the suicide bomber. He'd heard she was a teenage girl, thin, wearing glasses, walking stiffly in rubber sandals. Someone had seen her approach the clinic's door, evidently with explosives taped to her legs beneath her sari. One moment she had been standing on the front step, her hand raised as if about to knock. The next moment she and the clinic had vanished in a blast of dynamite.

"Why now?" the taxi-man asked, his voice rising. "Yesterday, every day—soldiers are everywhere guarding, round the clock. This morning, people say, no army is here. Not one soldier! Why?"

Richard shook his head. He and the man walked back toward the market in silence. Among the stalls now, Richard took a small towel from a stack and wiped Lila's wet face with it. She felt his hand behind the cloth gently moving along her nose, her lips, her eyes.

"I'll listen to my radio when we get back. We'll find out everything." Richard leaned over to speak into her ear.

"I want to go home," she said, her voice muffled.

"We'll take a taxi now," he said.

She nodded, but the world stayed dark. She gripped his hand, pushing it and the towel against her eyes. He didn't try to pull away; he just stood quietly beside her. She could hear him breathing now. Finally she released his hand. It fell away slowly. Raising her face, Lila blinked into the glare.

TWELVE

No one at home knew anything. Not Daya at the gate—he only gave her a strange look as she and Richard climbed out of the taxi. None of the bushes and palmettos and flowers along the driveway knew anything, or they wouldn't have glowed so glaringly bright around her, hurting her eyes with their insistent brightly colored ignorance. The house above the cricket pitch knew nothing, with its loud greenery clinging to the walls and moss cozily covering the roof.

But after several minutes standing on the front steps—dizzy with breathlessness, listening to the familiar pulse of the cicadas, and staring about at the lovely sanctuary—Lila thought: perhaps there's nothing to know, perhaps nothing's changed after all. Then she understood that she was what had changed. She smelled the sick smell of herself. She felt her mother scrubbing her school uniform with a wet cloth because she'd vomited all over her clothes in the taxi. Now her mother was helping her out of the wet white blouse and green skirt and knee socks.

"Can we burn them?" Lila asked, wiping her eyes. She pictured the trash pile behind the rubber-smoking shed where old coconut husks smoldered.

"We'll see. We can probably wash them," her mother said, pushing Lila's hand into the sleeve of a clean dress. "We haven't got that many uniforms."

"I won't need any more!" Lila expected her mother to disagree, soothingly, humorously, kneeling before her and saying, "Of course you will, silly—what do you think you're going to wear to school?" But though she did kneel and hold her by the sides, her fingers gripping her tightly, she just stared at Lila.

Finally she stood up and brushed Lila's hair away from her eyes. "We're going to listen to the noon news program from Colombo." Her voice had none of that forced cheeriness Lila had expected to argue against. "Maybe there'll be something about the Sharmas."

Papa was in the sitting room when she walked out; he leaned over, wrapped his arms around her. She felt his beard press against her cheek and she hugged his head, feeling his thick hair in her fingers. When he stood up, she saw from his eyes that he'd been taking the medicine, which let him get up from his bed but made him move and talk slowly.

"Thank heavens you're all right!" He held the sofa back for balance. "You shouldn't have had to see all that."

"I had to," she said, her voice sounding small and far away. "It was all there."

"But it's not here. *We're* all here," he said. "And *this* is here, too." He moved toward the wall next to the shelves where the biology texts were piled, and pointed to a paper framed on the wall. It was the letter from the Assistant Minister. Lila stood before it, but her eyes couldn't focus well enough to read the words. Sue and Richard stood where they were, not approaching the framed letter.

"How could it have *happened?*" Sue demanded from Derek, but he had no answer.

Lila's gaze fell on the leg of the dining room table. All the legs rested in clay saucers that held water; she or her mother filled them every day to keep the ants from crawling up and getting at whatever tiny crumbs might have been missed when the table top was wiped off. Now one of the saucers was dry, Lila noticed. But the ants hadn't found it yet. She ran to the table and, standing on tiptoe, reached across for the water pitcher. It was boiled water, for drinking, but she used it to fill the saucer anyway, then filled the other ones, too, because they were nearly dry. She expected her mother to scold her for using drinking water, but Sue just took the pitcher from her hand and carefully draped the cloth back over the top.

"We'll listen to the radio now," she said.

It was an old white plastic set with a round dial; Lila had once drawn it as a rectangular-cornered baby with a big pacifier. It was always set to the only station it picked up, the government service in Colombo. Today the two first items were about cabinet ministers travelling abroad. Then an announcement of the blast at Kaduwa did come on. The woman news-reader's voice speaking from the radio made it official, but not much different. A Tamil Tiger suicide bomber had blown up a small clinic, which fortunately had been closed at the time. Nonetheless, two people had been killed and seventeen people wounded in the blast.

Lila leaned over her mother's lap at the table to listen. "*Who* was killed?" she shouted at the radio.

"*The Minister for Defense stated…*" There were commentaries about the blast, about tighter security measures to be taken, about peace initiatives possibly jeopardized…but no names of the killed people were given. Lila heard a brief statement about an attack on a German hotel owner. It sounded like nothing much had happened, that perhaps someone had punched Hans or thrown a stone at him. Authorities were investigating. Then the announcer spoke about the decline in tourism for the month and began summarizing a cricket test match between Sri Lanka and Pakistan. Sue switched the radio off.

"That's all we get," she said, turning to Richard.

"It used to be enough." Derek spoke in a low voice.

Lila spotted Richard's black radio resting beside him on

the couch opposite, and rushed to snatch it up. "What's this one say?" she asked. "Can I try it?"

Richard nodded. "Sure. But nothing usually comes in till later in the afternoon."

He'd told her this before, and she expected her mother to say, "Put it down, dear." She thought her father would say, "You're wasting Richard's batteries, now turn it off." But everyone sat still, watching her. Today—perhaps because she'd seen the things the broadcast had reported—she seemed to have some authority; people were treating her almost like an adult. Very slowly she turned the little radio's black knob. All she heard was static that made her grit her teeth, then silence—on the radio, in the sitting room, outside, everywhere. She didn't stop turning the knob until Richard gently took the radio from her hands.

"We'll try later," he said. "Okay?"

Lila watched him push the switch to the "off" position. "Okay," she said, leaning against his knee. Like her, he knew everything that had happened this morning. "But what are we going to do now?"

He put the radio down. He'd changed his clothes, too, and wore a sarong with a long cotton shirt instead of jeans and his checked shirt. "We'll wait," he said. "And then we'll figure out something to do."

"Could you help me get lunch ready?" Sue asked Lila, standing up from the dining room chair. "I need someone to grate some coconut."

"How can we just…grate coconut?" Lila looked around the room. The couch, the table, the bookshelves, the framed watercolors she'd painted—so long ago!—of buffaloes and flowers: they were all there but something wasn't, something was missing.

"Have you seen Zalie?" she asked suddenly. When no one spoke, she asked again. "Was she on my bed this morning?" She couldn't remember, it seemed so long ago.

"Richard'll help you look for her this afternoon," her mother said finally.

"We'll find her," Richard said, leaning forward.

"But this afternoon we have to listen to the *radio!*" Lila suddenly screamed. She stumbled forward. Her father held her up, but she squirmed out of his grip. "I don't know what's happened to Zalie! I have to find her *now!*"

Then something strange happened. All three of them—Richard, her father, and mother—rushed to stop her. If they hadn't, she would have dashed out the front door and down the driveway. She was so surprised that anyone would keep her from going anywhere—actually holding her arms tight, moving her backwards from the doorway—that she just looked up at the faces around her without a sound. Finally she let herself be taken into the kitchen to help her mother make lunch.

The meal was eaten in silence, as if Mum and Papa and Richard were waiting for something, as if they didn't want to be speaking when news came rushing into the room. Lila wanted to talk, to describe again everything she'd seen, but she was familiar with these about-to-burst sensations and knew there were no words inside her to let them all out with. She'd have to draw or paint them.

So instead of searching for Zalie—the sun outside was much too hot, like a bonfire behind the palm fronds framed by her window—she drew in her room. Lines zigzagged across the paper, black and red, black and red. Broken red buildings, trees and bushes, adults and children—all appeared behind black crosshatching. She sat for a long time with her hands over her eyes until the picture finally leaked out of her mind. The scene was just a piece of paper now, at least for the time being, and she folded it away under the back of the pad. Then she drew a portrait of a plump-cheeked girl in a sari looking at a birthday cake. But when the candles appeared, the cake got singed with the flames—it developed icing so black that Lila could almost smell its stink. She folded that picture away, too, and lay down for a moment on her bed, her face resting on the blue pillow where Zalie usually curled up to sleep. She heard her father shouting into his cell phone, making a call to Colombo to an attorney and to an aunt. Her mother was shouting into the receiver, too. Then Lila closed her eyes and the voices faded out behind a slow rhythmic crosshatching in her mind.

When she woke—to a familiar chiming sound—she sat up, drenched in sweat, wondering why she wasn't at school. She'd put on her school uniform this morning—where was it? Then, rubbing her eyes, she heard the familiar English voice of the radio. The chimes were for the BBC Overseas Service; the voice was explaining things she needed to hear.

In the sitting room, her mother and Richard were on one couch, Derek was lying on the other one on his side, his knees over the edge. The radio was on the table between the couches. It talked about England, then said, "In South Asia today…" Here Richard and Sue sat forward, but the news was about Madras in India—where the program was being relayed from: water purification schemes, a new industrial park…. Derek sat up, damp-eyed, and learned toward the radio, too. "A bomb blast in a government clinic rocked the southern town of Kaduwa, Sri Lanka, this morning, killing two persons—"

"*Who?*" Lila shouted from her bedroom doorway.

Everyone turned to her. Her mother put her finger to her lips, then motioned for her to come sit between her and Richard. The radio was crackling. Richard tilted its aerial sideways until the voice flew out of the static again.

"...The Assistant Minister for Ecological Affairs was taken into custody shortly after the bomb explosion, an arrest that had been rumored imminent for days. The Assistant Minister has been linked with payoffs made to Tamil Tiger leaders. Though the government has made no statements, the payments were reportedly made to the Tamil insurgents to confine the fighting to the northern provinces, thus keeping the strife from the Assistant Minister's home constituency. An abbot of a local monastery, as well as a German hotel owner, who was attacked the same day as the bomb explosion, are being questioned about their involvement with the politician...."

Derek staggered to his feet and rocked slowly in place. "It's all right!" he said, his voice hoarse and blurry. "I can answer questions if the police come. It's not illegal to make campaign fund contributions."

"Contributions?" Richard asked, and switched off the radio.

"I've done nothing wrong!" Derek raised his face, as if speaking to someone floating above Sue's head. Standing up from the couch, she strode to the wall and snatched down the framed letter. Lila twisted round to watch her. Sue's arm snapped forward. She smashed the frame face-down onto the dining table. Lila, hearing the glass crunch— just like the glass breaking under her feet this morning, only louder—let out a cry. Richard's arm went around her. She pressed her face into his shoulder.

Her mother was back. "Sorry, dear," she said in a whispery voice. "I had to do that, though."

"It's done," Richard said. "Now will you start thinking about what I said?"

Lila looked from face to face. Her mother didn't answer the question. Richard rested his head back against the cushion, letting out a long breath.

Derek stepped forward and took Sue's hand. "I'm sorry. But I did what I had to do."

"I know you did," she said, staring at the floor.

"Once I started corresponding with that man, he put pressure on me. If I hadn't contributed—well, I had no way of knowing what might happen here."

"All right," Sue said. "But what are we going to do now, damn it?"

"We'll stay here. We're safe on our home ground."

Now Richard was on his feet, too. "The hell we are."

Lila clapped her hands over her ears. "You're all *fighting!*" she screamed. Her voice sounded like a shout under water, resonating all around her. She dropped her hands quickly but the silence went on—everyone had stopped talking at once again and stood at angles, motionless. She darted between her parents and rushed into her room. She swung the door shut. It crashed against the frame, sending reverberations along the floor that she could feel in the soles of her bare feet.

Light streamed in from the two windows on either side of her bureau, showing everything still where it had always been. The big picture of the Buddha was still taped to the wall beside the window. There were the clothes hanging in the almirah, the carved wooden deer on her desk, the tiny stone incense burner in the Buddha's niche on the window ledge. Zalie had once knocked the stone off, coming in through the security bars. Lila focused on the bars. Zalie, if she wanted to, could walk in and out through them, but they were too close together for Lila to crawl through, though she had as a small child. Now she was in a cage.

Of course, she didn't stay in it for long; her mother knocked after a while and came in, walking quietly, to sit with Lila on her bed. It was time for tea, then cricket/softball in the front yard, then dinner—squash and rice and plantains with pineapple for desert—then cards....

"How can we just keep doing these things?" Lila asked, sitting up.

"Because for now, we have to," her mother said. "It's how we live."

And so Lila understood that she had to keep on with her old life as if continuing it would bring it back, though she and everyone else knew this was impossible. The cricket/softball game outside was strange, everyone standing, waiting as the ball was bowled and hit, then running after it, shouting the usual things—but as a kind of echo of previous games played on other evenings. The light slanted in through the trees a sea-green color, and sometimes Lila pictured them all playing under water, moving with exaggerated motion, their voices undulating throughout the liquid. A murky ocean had flooded the place, but everyone was pretending they could breathe and talk and move beneath its surface. She pictured the flowers like anemones, the bushes like sprays of coral growing out of the reef-like ground. When she ran, she glided along the ocean floor like a fish.

Then she felt that she was reenacting old after-tea cricket matches because it was a way of making sure she would always remember them at some time in the future when she would no longer be playing them. It was almost as if she were looking back on what she was doing—at the exact moment when she was doing it. This made her so confused and sad as she played that she needed to wipe her eyes with her fist.

Playing cards after dinner gave her this feeling, too. The electric power was off again, so they played by the light of the kerosene lanterns. She kept score more neatly than usual, wanting to make sure it would be readable in the future. When Richard had last visited, she'd put the score-keeping notebook away carefully for his next visit, knowing she could take it out again whenever it was needed. But now she wasn't so sure she could do that. She started gazing around the room, fixing the location of everything in her mind. The light glared in its globe, almost silver along the glass, then softer around the couches where they all sat, quickly fading to shadow on the floor halfway to the dining table. Overhead, the Buddha's-birthday-streamers hung limp, barely visible, reminding her of a color picture she had seen—and once reproduced—of the tentacles of jellyfish hanging down in beautiful shades of purple. And so the water-look of the place came back, too, the air turned thick and strangely colored, and the voices were delayed as they left people's lips as if about to be silenced in mid-sentence. Years later, when she would paint the scene, the light in the room became the sepia tint of old photos in books, and all four card players, including herself, became long-ago figures, locked in one pose forever.

In bed that night, she once woke in the darkness and knew just what Hans must feel like, being partly blind. She could feel the acid burning away her eyes. Her mother heard her screams and rushed in and wiped her stinging tears away with a cool wet cloth. Lila got up and paced around the floor while her mother sat on the bed holding a flaming candle on a saucer. When Lila lay down again, she stared at the candle and repeated some mantras with her mother's soft voice in her ear until, the next thing she knew, the candle flame was gone and sunbeams were slanting through the flower petals outside her window.

She put on a school uniform, then saw herself in her mirror. She seemed to be looking back a day in time, as if staring through a glass at a girl who would have to see things she didn't want to see again. She took off the uniform quickly and put on an ordinary dress, a purple one Richard had once said he liked as they'd gone for one of their walks around the plantation. It was a dress that had nothing to do with yesterday. No one suggested that she go to school when she came out for breakfast. Whether she did or not seemed to be up to her; she was old enough to make these decisions now. This was because of what she'd done and seen.

At mid-morning, the red phone rang in the sitting room, its chirping sound bringing everyone out of their rooms at once. Derek snatched up the phone; his Colombo attorney was on the line. He told Derek not to leave the sanctuary yet because it might look as if he were trying to flee. "Let the police come to you, if they're going to," he said. Richard and Sue stood watching Derek along with Lila. Almost the moment he put down the phone, it rang again. This time it was Daya: he reported that an automobile mechanic was at the gate.

Derek seemed confused about this, but when Richard and Sue both spoke to him at once, he told Daya to let the man in. Then he went out to look at some fences that the watchman said had been tampered with during the night. Lila watched out her window as a turbaned Sikh got off his motorcycle beside the Land Rover. He and Richard pulled the dusty tarpaulin off the car's hood, along with vines so thick they had to be cut back with a knife that the mechanic took out of the toolbox strapped to the back of his motorcycle. As she drew on her pad, she heard the man grunting and hammering underneath the car. At one point, engine bits and rubber tubes lay all over the grass; by afternoon, they were back under the hood. Lila heard the engine coughing and finally starting. The Sikh said he didn't know how long the battery would hold its charge; it might have been left too long. Richard paid him in American dollars and he rode off, skidding on the bumpy surface of the drive.

Later, Lila heard Richard tell Sue, "Now we finally have a way out of here."

Sue said, "Right. But we can't go anywhere."

Lila continued crosshatching her paper. Richard and Sue's voices faded in and out from the kitchen. Richard's visa would expire soon, he said; Raquel would need him back if they were going to take over the tree nursery.

"You have to make up your mind, Suzy," he said once, but Lila heard no response from her mother.

That day, there was no more news on either radio about the bombing or the arrest of the Assistant Minister, but Daya, who Mum said was much better than a radio, reported that over a dozen policemen and soldiers had spent the day ransacking Hans's hotel and digging up the gardens and tennis court and even the swimming pool. Some plastic bags of heroin and several pistols had been found. Hans had been treated at a Colombo hospital. In one eye, almost no vision remained, in the other, he could see about half as well as before. He had been returned to his hotel and placed under "protective custody." Two servants had come back; every day they searched the place hoping to find things that the army might have missed. They wore Hans's wristwatches and gold chains, claiming he'd given them out as gifts. Meenu was living at the hotel again, taking care of Hans.

"You'd think the government would deport him," Sue said at dinner. "Wouldn't you?"

Richard glanced at Derek, then put his fork down as he spoke. "If the government wants to make a case against the Assistant Minister, they'll want Hans around to give testimony."

"What's 'testimony'?" Lila asked.

No one rushed to answer her. Her father and mother and Richard were all looking down at their plates. Finally her mother spoke.

"Testimony means to say what you know in court," she said. "To be a witness."

"Am I a witness?" Lila leaned forward. "I saw what happened to Hans."

Her parents told her no, that was not what the government needed witnesses for, but Lila couldn't get the idea of appearing in court out of her head. At Radha's house she'd seen a television program in which a witness had been threatened if he said what he knew. Now she remembered the men who had run out of the Sports Haus gate; the small man with hair falling to his forehead had looked straight at her out of his burning, dark eyes. He knew what she looked like. Would he come after her to blind her, now?

The next morning, when she left the house, she borrowed from Richard the sunglasses he had brought with him but had hardly ever put on. She had to wind adhesive tape around the stems to make them stay on. When she looked at the road through them, it appeared not only darker but quieter than usual. Several military vehicles rolled by slowly, the soldiers staring straight ahead as if they saw something in the distance that no one else did. Zalie came back long enough to eat the food set out for her, then ran off again and Lila couldn't catch her. That afternoon Lila refused to take the sunglasses off at tea, though she knocked over the sugar bowl at the table. No one scolded her. Her mother silently went to the kitchen to get a wet rag. Lila helped her clean up the mess; she knew that even with saucers of water under the table legs, ants would find a way to get at spilled sugar.

Her father had tried to phone people he knew in Kaduwa but still hadn't been able to learn what had happened to the Sharma family. Daya hadn't heard anything, either, but he'd reported to Derek that Hans had started shooting off pistols in his range, even though he couldn't see very well. One of his men rolled bottles across the ground, and he tried to hit them by listening to the sounds they made. Cooking oil tins were swung from tree limbs; Hans blazed away, and sometimes a clanging noise was heard when a bullet actually hit a tin. The soldiers and policemen, drunk on Hans's liquor, thought this was amusing to watch—until Hans tried to jump into his jeep and drive off, pointing his gun at them. They managed to disarm him and wrestled him out of the vehicle, but soon he was staggering around the place with another pistol—he had them hidden everywhere—and threatened to escape again.

"Why do we have to keep talking about *Hans?*" Lila screamed. "What about Radha?"

Again, everyone looked at her, but no one scolded her. Finally Richard spoke.

"Tell you what, Lila. How about if I drive you to school tomorrow in the Land Rover? Then you could get some news, and I'll drive you back after your classes."

Lila took off her sunglasses for a moment. "Is that all right?" she asked, looking at her father, then her mother.

"Excellent," Derek said. "Back to school. We'll start normal life again."

Sue glanced at him, then turned to Lila. "It's a good idea, dear."

Lila smiled for the first time in days. But she put the glasses on again. They made her lose badly at rummy, not being able to tell clubs from spades sometimes, but nobody seemed to care who won or lost; the point was to keep the game going.

*

The next morning she wore the glasses with her school uniform. Richard had to sweep beetles out of the Land Rover before she got in. Today, he said, he was going to get some petrol, which he called "gas," and buy a battery charger, since the engine was hard to start up. Lila hadn't been in the car for over a year. Riding down the road, past the familiar houses and trees and paddy fields, she could almost feel normal again except that Richard was driving instead of her father. She was seeing an outdated life from a year ago, darkened today by her glasses. But she did like bouncing along the road with Richard. This time, he didn't make the wrong turn at the V and drove straight to the crossroads.

The market was crowded with people again; the usual spicy smells and haggling sounds rose from the stalls, and until Lila looked in the direction of the clinic, she found it hard to believe that anything had changed here. Then she saw the big chunks of concrete lying all over the ground. No one had removed anything except the furniture from the Sharmas' house. It looked like a big white storage carton tipped on its side, its compartments completely empty. Then Richard accelerated past the house to the brick church, with its little spire and colored windows, and the long cinder-block buildings that made up the school beside it.

He walked up the steps into the building with her to find out about the Sharmas. The rooms smelled of floor wax, as always, and held a dim light that slanted in through small windows set high in the walls. Nuns and Christian lay teachers in Western dresses were rushing along the corridors; today, apparently, was the first day that the school had been open since the bombing, and all the adults seemed confused. There were few girls anywhere. Lila stopped the first teacher who came out of the office, Sister Agnes, who taught maths. She was one of the few nuns who still wore a wimple, a pudgy-faced Irish woman with rimless spectacles and a big wooden cross resting on her bosom.

"Please Sister, where's Radha?" Lila asked her.

"Gone to Canada, I'm afraid," the nun said. She took Richard and Lila into an empty classroom and sat them down at desks to explain what had happened. Radha and Dr. Sharma, she said, had been burned in the blast and taken to a hospital in Colombo. But the school had received word that they were recovered well enough to travel, and the family was flying to Toronto to join relatives who had immigrated there a year ago.

"You must be relieved to know that Radha and her mother and father are all right," the nun said, watching Lila's face.

Lila nodded, sniffling. She took the white handkerchief the teacher gave her and wiped her eyes with it. "But I'll never see Radha again. How can she be just *gone?*"

"It's hard to believe, I know," the sister said. "I'm sorry. She was your best friend, wasn't she?"

"She still is."

"Of course, dear."

Richard asked Lila if she wanted to stay at school—she actually had the choice!—or see to the Land Rover with him. It was hard to make up her mind, but she decided she was too curious about what school would be like today to miss it. Then she regretted her choice, because in her first class, the desk where Radha had sat with her in the back was empty—like more than half the ones here—and she had no one to whisper with. The teacher tried to continue a history lesson from the previous week, but the girls were too busy staring around them at vacant places to pay attention.

Between classes, girls talked frantically about who had come back and who had left. They didn't rag each other much; you couldn't tell when someone might suddenly leave, and you didn't want to be the last person to say something nasty to a girl. Lila stopped hearing about her blue eyes; no one compared her to blue-eyed American film actresses. It made Lila feel strange, not even being teased.

Ama, a Moslem girl who'd always kept her head covered with beautiful scarves, had moved to Colombo with her family when the local branch of the national bank, where her father had worked, was shut down. Lydia, a Christian girl with round glasses, and Menika, a Buddhist Sinhalese girl who stuttered, both left the area almost overnight when their fathers, military officers, had been given new assignments. At least ten other Sinhalese girls were absent today, and so was the one Sikh student. Out of about a hundred students, sixteen had been Tamils; today only two older Tamil girls, Radhika and Mira, were at school. Dressed in identical green and white uniform saris, they stayed together in one corner of the yard during the break, refusing teachers' efforts to get them to play netball.

They sat together in chapel, too, while the Mother Superior asked divine assistance for the absent students. Girls who had never even moved their lips in these prayers joined in today, but Lila remained silent, not even whispering to anyone throughout the service. Two girls' fathers and one girl's brother—all were soldiers—were missing in action after a recent battle near Jaffna, the Mother Superior said; the uncle of another girl had been killed in a battle only seventy miles north, though the front was supposed to be well over a hundred miles away. Announcements like these had never been made in chapel before, though news of girls' families had circulated informally around the school. Lila was so confused by the chapel service that she couldn't do any of the maths problems she was given in the next class. No one else could, either; Sister Agnes finally did them herself on the board for everyone to copy into their notebooks.

Classes continued into the afternoon: the "hippopotamuses" of triangles were measured (no one laughed at the teacher's old joke). Capital cities of the world's nations were recited, almost screamed, in unison, rattling the glass in the windows; Browning's *Last Duchess* smiled forever innocent from her portrait on her wall. In the final period, a study hall, Lila kept all her books ready in her knapsack, staring out the window for Richard's car. As soon as she saw the Land Rover pull up to the school, she ran from her desk. In the corridor she heard the final bell clanging from the main office.

Usually at least a dozen shiny sedans waited for girls at the end of the school day. Now only four were outside, their drivers no longer napping behind the wheels but standing sharply beside the car doors keeping a lookout for their charges. The girls taking the bullock-cart bus—service had resumed again—no longer kept the driver waiting as they gossiped in the halls, but burst out of the school doors and climbed aboard quickly. Lila ran past them and swung herself up into the front seat of the Land Rover.

"No more sunglasses," Richard said, smiling at her as he leaned forward to turn the ignition key.

"I've got them in my pocket."

"That's good. You can keep them as long as you want." The engine started up. Richard adjusted the brim of his hat. "How was school?"

"Too strange!" She was still out of breath. "I want to go home!"

Richard shifted into gear. "Where nothing's strange," he said.

She leaned toward him in her seat, unsure she'd heard him clearly over the engine noise. Then, as the car shot forward, she had to grab the dashboard to keep from tipping off her seat.

"What?" she cried.

"Never mind." He steadied her with his hand on her arm. "We're going home."

THIRTEEN

The long rains began after weeks of mostly dry, glaring sunshine. The earth sucked up water so thirstily that Lila could almost hear the slurping and sighing of plants all around the house. With vertical strokes of her silver pastel crayon she sketched the rain pouring past the windows, which expanded to three times their normal size because of the huge noise that gushed through them. She'd never heard a monsoon like this before. The clatter on the ceiling became insistent, trying to shout something whose words she could never quite make out. She drew open mouths tapping their teeth against the roof tiles, alphabet letters leaking through and splattering onto the floor. The house shrank and became confining, since few people opened any doors or went outside; at the same time, the rooms seemed larger because you had to shout across them to be heard through the racket. Zalie was gone more and more often, as if pulled mysteriously outdoors. The weather made it hard for Lila to go look for her, though she tried every day.

Usually Lila liked to draw on the sitting room couch; it was the best place in the house for overhearing conversations. But nowadays she heard only parts of them. Sue and Richard talked to each other quietly. Her mother and father spoke loudly, shouted sometimes, but ended sentences part way through and walked away in different directions. Her father and Richard seemed not to talk at all. She could hear everyone speaking directly to her, of course, but what was said didn't always make sense. Years later, she would remember the strange questions all three adults asked her during these long, last days.

Shall we whitewash some rocks down by the gate? her father asked her. But the whitewash would come right off when the rain started up again, she replied. Well, he meant later— some other time—soon. He laughed his rumbly laugh. Lila said: Okay, she'd help.

Rummy tonight? Richard asked her. But the evening before, he'd said he needed a few nights off from the cards because he'd started dreaming about big cards in the gardens like the ones in *Alice in Wonderland*. Lila said she'd play rummy again.

Can you help me iron your uniform? her mother asked her, but Lila had already shown her the printed notice the school had mailed her saying it would be shut while teachers "reorganized classes to accommodate smaller enrollment." If we iron the uniform now, Lila said, it'll just get damp from the rains. Oh, right, her mother said, shaking her head, we'll wait.

Everyone worried about keeping her busy. Then, strangely, when there was something to do—getting the rubber ready to sell—her father said it was too dirty a job for her to help with. All day the smell of smoked rubber drifted through the windows, stinging Lila's eyes. Standing out in the drizzly kitchen courtyard, she caught glimpses of red charcoal glowing between the black slats of the smoke-house wall. Crunch! Crash! Women threw armloads of branches and coconut husks onto the fire around back. Inside the shed her father and the men were processing sap into rubber, and that night black rectangular sheets the size of car floor-mats would hang on racks to cool. When enough cooled mats were stacked up on the shelves, a truck would come up the driveway to take them to the market. At least this was how it happened every year.

Her father walked into the courtyard wearing only an old pair of cotton trousers. His hair and beard were wild and his face was smudged as if by dark paint. He hosed himself off and walked into the kitchen wearing a clean sarong and white shirt.

"It's the best crop in years," he said to Lila. Her mother came out and handed him a glass bottle; leaning back, he poured water into his mouth without touching the rim to his lips. Finally he stood straight. His eyes were damp, the pupils dilated. "We'll have a real income again. Enough to finish the cages, to put borders around the gardens...." Sue took the bottle from him, smiling vaguely, silent. Lila stared at her. Maybe she remembered, as Lila did, that only a few days ago Papa had said that the price of rubber was so low this year that it hardly paid to harvest it.

Later that night he said, "I think I'm going to chop the trees down—timber prices are high now."

Then Richard, who loved trees—naturally, since he was buying a nursery—said, "Once you cut them down, they're gone forever."

"In a sanctuary, we want wild things growing—habitats for wild creatures."

"The place is already filling up with wild creatures," Richard said. "Two-legged ones."

"We've got very good security!" Derek lowered his chin to glare at Richard.

"I've seen fresh footprints on a lot of the paths. And tire tracks," Richard said. "Lila's seen them, too."

Her mother leaned forward. "Richard, don't you put her in this position—*don't!*"

"You saw the tire tracks, yourself, Sue. I showed you the ones by the north gate," Richard said.

Sue turned away. "They must have been made by our own people."

Richard put down his fork, keeping his hand on it as if to prevent it from jumping up from the table. "And how many of them drive motorcycles with brand-new tires?"

"Our people could have had visitors." Sue refilled her glass from the pitcher, then leaned across the table toward Lila. "Would you like some more, dear?"

"Thank you." Lila watched her glass fill up. But she wasn't thirsty. She wanted to speak up about the tracks she'd seen leading to one of the old outbuildings. But maybe the footprints and tire tracks really were made by workers or their friends. And maybe her father was right about the security—he'd been stringing wire everywhere for days, even in the rain. She glanced at him. The way he was looking at Richard made her look down again, silent. She wished she knew where her cat was.

Later, she watched Richard writing in his journal at the empty table, and heard her father scratching away in his office as he drew up new plans for the sanctuary. She remembered something her father had once told her last year, before this trouble started. All plantations, he'd said, have to put up with a certain number of squatters; no matter how hard you try to keep them out, a few always get in; but if they stay awhile, some of them make very good workers. I think people need a sanctuary, too, he'd told her.

At dinner, if she'd reminded him that he'd said that…no, maybe it wasn't a good time to bring up squatters. At breakfast tomorrow, perhaps….

But the next morning, she found her mother leaning over the kitchen counter with tears streaming down her cheeks. Lila rushed in. Sue made low moaning sounds. Derek stood beside her, his eyes burning, lines pulled tight across his forehead. He gripped her arm, trying to tell her something; she shook her head, her tangled hair flapping back and forth. In the kitchen corridor Richard beckoned for Lila to come into the sitting room with him.

"Last night, someone stole the rubber mats from the smoke house," he told her, his voice low. "About half the crop. This could be the last straw."

Lila sat down hard on a dining room chair. "*Who* stole it?"

"Nobody knows. It's never happened before."

Lila squinted around the room, feeling her heart thumping fast in her chest. So many things were going on that had never happened before. The rain had stopped; the house seemed to be holding its breath, waiting for something more. The only sounds were the low voices from the kitchen. Then they faded, as Derek and Sue went out into the courtyard, probably to talk to some of the workers about the theft. The police, of course, couldn't be called.

"What are we going to do now?" Lila asked, her voice sounding choked and strange.

Richard poured himself a glass of water from the pitcher and stood staring at it. He was wearing his jeans and boots and checked shirt, looking very American today. His hair was pulled back so tight it surely must hurt his forehead. Lila wanted to reach behind his head and loosen the elastic band that held his ponytail, but she visualized his hair flying out in all directions, even his brains exploding through his scalp, if anyone touched his hair—that was how tense he looked. She watched him drink the water and replace the cloth over the pitcher. He breathed evenly with a rhythm that reminded her of the meditation exercises that

Sue had taught him two years ago to keep him calm; he must be remembering them now.

"Well, for now…" he gazed out the window. "Let's you and me go for a walk before the rain starts again."

"Okay." Lila jumped to her feet. "First I want to make a phone call—just to Daya."

"Is Zalie missing again?"

"Yes—again!" Lila rushed into her room to get her cell phone. Daya answered on the first ring and went to look in the little hut where Zalie liked to stay, the same lean-to shelter that Lila had made out of the palm fronds on the day Richard had arrived. Daya was back quickly; he had orders not to leave his observation post on the platform, he said. He'd phone her immediately, he promised, if any cat entered the area.

*

Years later, when Lila remembered her terrible last walk to the sanctuary's zoo, she recalled that the afternoon had suddenly turned fresh and clear, even beautiful. She'd chosen the zoo for a destination because she had to be sure that Zalie wasn't back in the cage. That wasn't likely, but she had to stop picturing Zalie gazing up at her from behind the wire fence.

She strapped her canvas knapsack on and dropped in her cell phone, in case Daya might call. She also slipped in the postcard of Sakajawea and her white horse. Lila wondered, could you ride a horse in the snow, or did its bare feet get too cold? Having cold feet was supposed to mean you were scared; Lila had never had cold feet, yet she'd been scared sometimes.

The sunlight glittered in the wet foliage as if all the landscape had been sprayed with glass beads. She watched the wet drops slide off leaves and make a pattern on the back of Richard's shirt. The long grass soaked the cuffs of his jeans. He inhaled long breaths of the warm air as he walked; she watched him smile when his boots made a slurping sound in a muddy indentation. She stepped in it, too, her own rubber sandals turning to red-brown sponges beneath her soles, and she felt the wet earth squishing between her toes.

"I can see why your father never wants to leave here," Richard said, "especially when things look like this." He waved his hand in the air. As if in response, a flock of parrots swooped out of a gum tree, green flecks spiraling up into the pale blue sky. He watched them glide out of sight above the tree tops. "All these lovely colors and sounds," he said. "I'll miss them."

"Do you have to go back soon?" Lila asked.

"Soon, yeah." He sighed. "But I keep waiting...."

Lila took his hand. She was conscious of their footsteps landing on the earth in unison. "If I went to visit you," she said suddenly, "I mean, one day—do you think Raquel would teach me to ride one of her horses?"

"Sure!" Richard grinned, slowing his pace. "She'd have you riding all over the mountains with her in no time."

"Mountains with snow on them, like in the postcard?"

"All the snow you want."

Lila pressed her lips together to keep herself from thinking about the mountains too vividly. Once she'd visited a great-aunt's tea estate in the high hills near Nuwara Eliya; the road had wound up and up, past waterfalls that hung from crags like silver hair, past sloping fields where Tamil women with jute sacks waded through tea groves, picking the leaves. Now she pictured the women in their saris wading through snow, filling their bags with the beautiful white fluff. The whole hillside was pure white as far as she could see. No gray smoke rose from thieved smoke-houses; no cement rubble lay about, singed with ugly black streaks. The fluff fell from the sky like white blossoms and covered everything. It made a soft sound as it fell, muffling the explosions of bombs far away at the bottom of the valley. The noises were so distant that you forgot them forever and just heard the murmur of women's voices floating in a mist along the slope. She pictured Radha among the women; somehow she was grown up now, plump like her mother, and Lila was grown, too, tall and strong and wearing a buckskin dress with tassels like Sakajawea's. Lila was riding toward Radha on her horse whose feet never got cold. Radha waved to her, and when the horse stopped, she climbed up behind Lila and they rode away through the white fluff toward the house where Richard and Raquel lived on the other side of the mountain.

Years later, she would think how strange it had been to visualize snow while she was walking through a hot, green, tropical landscape whose details she would ache to remember. As she walked now, though, she just thought of the white vision as a picture to store away in her mind. Tonight, she decided, she'd try drawing it.

"You think about that visit to Colorado," Richard said, bending down to look her in the eye. A trace of a grin was still there, but his gaze was intense, his brow furrowed with the two vertical lines. "Because we've got to make plans very soon."

Around her the insects kept buzzing, throbbing louder and louder in the damp air. Lila now tried to will the phone to ring in her knapsack, so they could avoid going to the zoo. They could run down the drive to the gate, instead, to see Daya holding the cat in his arms. But the phone stayed silent, and she walked on. This time, if Zalie was in the zoo, Lila would let her out. She wouldn't ask anyone's permission; she didn't have to do that anymore.

At the top of a rise, she could see the stormy part of the sky where the rain was lingering—retreating or advancing, she couldn't tell. A long red streak appeared in the gray, as the clouds opened like a dark fabric being torn open to reveal its lining. Lila heard her own breaths as she walked on, and felt cool droplets of water trickling down her neck from overhanging leaves. She wanted to go more slowly or even stop, yet the sloping terrain was making her walk fast along the widening path, and she wished she hadn't let go of Richard's hand. Now she could see the row of cement bases, the two wire cages at the end looking smaller than she had remembered them.

The gate of the first cage was open; inside, in the tiny jungle of glossy-leafed weeds, no cat appeared. "Zalie's not here!" Lila tried to laugh with relief, but her voice felt choked. The cage looked ugly, chaotic, overgrown; it was damp and dark; it wasn't even safe—its walls were just wire, its gate nothing but a piece of metal.

Richard stood several paces ahead of Lila on the path past the cages. He wiped his forehead with the bandana he pulled from his back pocket. "Good," he said. "She's somewhere else. How's the turtle?"

"I'll look."

Richard took a step back. Then he nearly stumbled over something and looked down. "Oh, *hell!*"

"What's the matter?"

"Lila—don't come closer!—"

But it was too late. She saw it. Right in the middle of the path, just past the cages, the cat lay sprawled on its belly.

Her hind feet were collapsed in the mud. Lila suddenly smelled a sour odor. The sounds of water dripping seemed to stop, creating silence everywhere. She saw a line of ants crawling up an open red gash in Zalie's fur where, in the middle of her back, the handle of a knife was buried. Its long blade had pinned the cat to the ground.

Lila sank to her knees. The cat's fur was still silky and damp when she touched it. But the flesh beneath it was cold. When she tried to move Zalie's head, the cat's entire body—stiff, now—shifted in the mud. Black ants crawled over Lila's knuckles. "Ay!" she cried, and shook them off hard. A sickening, sour odor rose to her nostrils. She buried her face in her hands. "*Zalie!*"

Richard knelt beside her, his arm going around her shoulder. "I'm so sorry."

"Why did they kill her?" she asked, her voice cracking.

Richard's jaw was clamped tight. He shook his head.

"Somebody thought she was possessed, maybe," Lila said.

"Maybe."

"It's not fair!" Lila cried.

"No—it's not."

Lila rubbed her eyes. "We have to bury her. We have to have a ceremony."

"A ceremony would be good." Richard stared at the cat, then turned to look down the path toward the house. "But I don't think there's time. We've got to leave."

"Now?"

Richard nodded. "Go look at the turtle. Go on, just for a minute."

Lila rose and took a wobbly step forward, then another. Thomas was still in his cage. He lay on a flat rock, his shell gold and black in the pale glowing light.

"Your friend's dead," Lila whispered, stooping over.

She didn't expect the tortoise to respond, but he did, tilting his ancient beaked face toward her. She reached down and tugged out the wooden peg that fastened the latch of his gate. Behind her she heard the sounds of the knife blade scraping and digging. She couldn't look back, not yet.

"Go on, Thomas." She pulled open his gate. The tortoise didn't move. Lila stood up straight, tears rolling down her cheeks. "The door's open," she said. "You're free."

The tortoise blinked slowly and took a step forward.

Lila turned around. Richard had dug a hole in the mud among some yellow-flowering weeds. Now, still kneeling, he set Zalie's body in the hole with both hands.

"Say something, Lila." He glanced up at her.

She stepped closer. She'd never buried anything before or been to a funeral. *"The jewel is in the blossom of the lotus,"* she whispered. The cat looked as if she were sleeping on her side now, the gash out of sight. "When you come back next time, Zalie…" Lila pressed her knuckles to her lips. She tasted the salt of her tears.

Richard spoke. "Maybe she'll be a girl, next time."

"Or a deer or—or a horse," Lila said.

"Amen," Richard said, and pushed some wet earth into the hole.

Lila knelt and, cupping her hands, helped him to bury her cat.

FOURTEEN

"No! *No!*" Sue cried, staring at the knife. She pressed her hand to her mouth, squeezing her eyes shut tight. Then she wrapped her arms around Lila. As Richard told her what had happened, Lila leaned her face against her mother. The soft cotton blouse with its familiar scent of laundry soap absorbed some of her tears but couldn't soak up the dull pain she could feel all through her body. She saw the knife lying in the bandana in Richard's open palm. Its steel blade was shiny; the long wooden handle looked like a miniature truncheon.

Richard reached out and rested his free hand against Sue's cheek. "We have to go today, Suzy—right now," he said. "The car's working. It's time!"

"Today?" Sue let out a long breath. "Perhaps…"

"Today!" Richard said.

"Where can we go?" Lila asked. Her voice scraped out of her throat.

"I suppose…Colombo." Sue sniffled hard. "Then, we'd have to see…."

"What about Papa?"

"If he'll come—" Sue shook her head.

"We've got to pack now," Richard said. "We can be ready, no matter what he says."

"I don't know…."

Richard turned Sue's chin so that she had to stare straight at the knife. Then he moved her face so that she was gazing down at Lila. "It might have been her," he said.

"Yes," Sue whispered. "Yes, all right."

Lila, still leaning against her, stared up at her face. "Why did they kill Zalie?"

"To show us they can get in here—as close to us as they want," Sue said.

"Who did it?" Lila asked.

"Refugees, Tamil Tigers, government soldiers—it could have been anyone—" Her mother shook her head hard, her eyes damp behind her lenses. "Once I thought I knew this place so well! It's our home! But I don't know what's happened to it!"

"Sue—come on!" Richard said.

"Right!" She cleared her throat and loosened her grip on Lila. "Go get your clothes out, dear. I'll come help you pack in a moment."

In her room, Lila pulled handfuls of underwear from her bureau drawers and flung them onto her bed. She felt dizzy as she moved, but she had to do something to keep the hurt from rising up her throat. Should she bring her school uniform? She took it out of the almirah and dropped it on the bed, too. Then she sat down hard. She pictured Zalie staring up as someone raised the knife and stabbed it down fast, pinning the cat to the ground, alive—for how long? A few seconds, a minute, several minutes? Had she cried out in pain—made that insistent mewing? Nobody had heard her—she'd been alone on the path. She thrashed furiously in place; she scrabbled her feet against the dirt, straining to push herself up. Her sight dimmed; her legs moved more and more slowly; the strength left them until finally, deep inside, she collapsed. Finally the mewing stopped. And the silence fell, spreading over her, blocking out the foliage, the earth, the light.

Sue found Lila sitting on the bed near the pile of clothes with her drawing pad open to a blank page on her lap. She tried to take the pad, but Lila wouldn't let go of it and wouldn't stop staring at the blank page. Finally Sue lifted down a canvas duffel from the top of the almirah and began pushing clothes into the zippered opening.

"We'll put the pad in your knapsack," she said.

Lila looked up, realizing she was still wearing the almost empty backpack. The cell phone was still inside it. She took it out, stuffed in her pad and colored pencils, and wedged the phone back in beside them. A clattering began overhead. The rains were starting again.

The front door slammed. Derek was back. Lila and Sue met him in the sitting room.

"Just made it!" he muttered, glancing up. His white bush shirt was splattered with raindrops. He moved toward the bedroom, his fingers pressed against his forehead.

"I've got to show you something!" Sue pointed at the table where the knife still lay on Richard's bandana.

But Derek didn't see it. He was at his bureau, reaching into his top drawer. "Give me five minutes before lunch," he said, out of breath. He found a little bottle, yanked the cork with his teeth and spat it out. Then he upended the bottle between his lips. Still gripping it in his hand, he dropped onto his side on the bed, his knees drawn up to his chest, eyes shut tight.

Sue pulled Lila into the kitchen. "We may as well eat something fast. I'll heat the rice." Sue opened the fridge to pull out a pot. "Chop up those tomatoes, will you?"

Lila's hand stopped in midair. She'd used the old chopping knife hundreds of times, but today she couldn't touch it. "I don't want any tomatoes."

"Lila, just help me—" Sue picked up a tomato. She looked as if she were going to squeeze the juice out of it. "All right, light the gas ring, dear."

Lila picked up the box of matches. When the power was off, as it was now, her mother used a cooker attached to a metal cylinder of gas. Lila struck a match but a damp wind from the window blew it out immediately. The rain was louder outside the bars; it said *"shhhhhhh"*—the opposite of what she wanted to do.

"What's Richard doing?" Her voice still sounded ragged.

Sue shook the hair from her face. "He's packing."

Lila struck another match. It, too, fizzled out as soon as she moved it near the gas ring. "Papa has to come with us!" she said. "It has to be *all* of us!"

Sue took the matchbox gently from Lila's hand. "Richard and I are going to talk to your father," she said. "Go finish filling up your duffel. You don't have to take everything."

"Will we ever come back here?"

Sue turned away, sliding open the matchbox. "Oh, I think so." Suddenly she dropped the box. Matches skidded all over the floor. She made a cry, something between a sob and a sigh, and stared down at them.

Lila knelt and began picking them up. Sue joined her, squatting on the stone floor with one arm around Lila's waist—to steady her, or steady herself, Lila couldn't tell. Then Lila hurried to her room. She heard Richard's radio talking, but the rain's clatter on the roof made it impossible to understand. Lila began stuffing clothes into the duffel bag. She hung the school uniform up in the almirah again, smoothing out the green tie. When her mother called her from the dining area, she left the duffel and the knapsack on the bed.

The rice was scorched, the tomatoes were sour, and the piles of leftover coconut curry on each plate were cold. But it was lunch; every day the family ate lunch together; it was necessary. Lila chewed a few mouthfuls, then gave up, feeling queasy. Richard's chair scraped against the floor as he sat down beside her, facing Derek. She watched him reach out to his rolled-up bandana on the table.

"Derek, listen to me," he said. The exclamation marks rose up his forehead, but his voice was quiet. "Someone came in and killed the cat last night or this morning." He unwrapped the knife from the bandana and pushed it toward Derek. "This is what they killed her with."

Derek turned slowly toward Richard. His eyes were glassy again, his pupils dilated, but he took in the expression on Richard's face and then looked down at the knife. It was an old one with a polished wooden handle and a blade about five inches long. Lila could see that the blade had recently been sharpened; scratch marks swirled in the steel toward the thin, sharp point.

"This is a good knife," Richard said. "Nobody'd leave it behind without a reason."

"It's a sign, like that bottle fetish!" Sue leaned forward.

Derek picked up the knife, running his finger along the side of the blade. "Poor Zalie," he said, and glanced at Lila. "I'm very sorry, *pol*."

Lila pushed her knuckles against her lips and stared back at him, hurting again.

"It's not just 'Poor Zalie,'" Sue said.

"It's a message." Richard turned to Derek. "How much do I have to spell out for you?"

Derek dropped the knife. Holding the table's edge, he lurched to his feet. The chair tilted, then crashed over backwards. "You don't have to come here and spell anything out to me about—about running my sanctuary!"

Richard stood up, too. "I'm telling you—we have to leave here. Now! Today!"

Derek shook his head slowly. "We can increase security. We've got wire fencing—"

"Wire!" Sue said, her voice sounding like a quiet scream.

"I can't *leave* here, Sue!" Derek suddenly roared. "It'll look like I'm fleeing!"

"What does that matter now?"

"I can't abandon all this! How can I?"

"We're leaving," Richard said, staring at Derek. "Sue and Lila and me."

"You come here—you think you can take my wife and my daughter off with you!" Derek tilted forward and snatched up the knife. "Get out, if you want to—but—"

"No!" Sue shouted, half rising from her chair.

Lila reached out. "Papa—"

Derek's arm snapped forward. The knife did a fast spin in the air and stuck into the table in front of Richard. It quivered, then went still. Now the only sound in the room was the rain hissing at the windows, clattering on the roof.

Then Lila heard the room fill with voices, everyone shouting, asking questions. They swirled around her like *preta* spirits. She could feel their cold breath against her cheeks, hear their demonic laughter cackling in the air. When she looked at her father's face, she could see that he heard them, too.

"*You never believed in the sanctuary!*" he shouted at Richard.

"I believed in it, Derek!" Richard tilted forward. "For all those months I was here last time, I believed in it like I

never believed in anything before! For two years afterwards, when I had nothing else to keep me going—I *believed*
in it. I believed in Lila and Sue, and in you!" Richard wiped
his forehead. His voice went quiet again, almost a whisper.
"But now we've got to leave."

Derek shook his head, and for a moment, his eyes closed
in tight half-moons. Then he tugged at his beard and took a
long breath. "I'm going to go check the security at the gate,"
he said, and turned toward the door.

"Papa, we have to all agree!" Lila cried out. "We have to
stay *together!*"

But her voice was drowned out by the rain. Its noise
ricocheted between ceiling and floor. A blast of wet wind
flew through the windows, snapping the curtains. Her
father was gone. For a long moment, Lila stayed at the
table. Richard said something about loading the Land
Rover. Sue asked if they could wait until the rain stopped.

"No." Richard moved toward his room. "We'll pick up
Derek at the gate if we can—"

Suddenly Lila didn't feel the *preta* swirling around the
room any longer. She scrambled to her feet. She didn't even
hear her mother's voice, or Richard's, as she ran toward the
door. Nor did she hear the ringing that came from the
knapsack on the bed in her room.

*

Years later, Lila wondered: what would have happened if
she'd heard the phone, and had listened to Daya speaking
from his post at the gate? Would she have waited and gone
down the driveway in the car with her mother and
Richard? She never knew, and the questions would
continue to swirl together in the memory of her childhood
home like echoes in an old, abandoned aviary.

If she hadn't run out into the rain, Lila later learned, she would have heard Daya saying on the phone that Hans was at the gate in his Jeep, bare to the waist in long canvas trousers and shouting in a high, hoarse voice. A raw red wound covered one side of his face; his eyes were cloudy, mad with pain and drugs. On the phone, Sue heard the incessant honking, honking, honking of the Jeep's horn.

"Let me in!" Hans screamed up at Daya, who was watching him from the platform above the steel gate. "They will kill me! *Give me sanctuary!*"

Lila heard nothing but the splashing of the rain in the bushes as she dashed down the driveway. One sandal went flying as she pitched forward, then both her feet were bare. She skidded as a wire gate rose up before her—in the downpour, she had turned onto the path beside the drive, and now she had to fumble with the latch to get through. Water streamed down her face, and she cut her finger on one of the barbs, but she was through.

"Should I let Hans in?" Daya was shouting into the phone to Sue as he paced on his platform.

"No! No!" Sue shouted back.

"I see Mr. Gunasekera coming. If he tells me to let the German in, I must do it!" Daya cried.

Lila stumbled on down the path, the rain shouting in her ears. The wire-bordered false path sloped off to the left, its barbs dripping rain. She saw the seedlings she'd labeled a few weeks earlier. She recognized the spot on the path where Zalie had killed the baby squirrel and left it behind. Here she slipped in a big puddle and had to grab a signpost to keep her balance. She'd painted the sign herself: *EXHIBITS THIS WAY*, but already the letters were nearly washed off. Pushing herself up, Lila rushed on again, the mud flying around her feet.

And now she heard crashing sounds ahead, though she had no idea what was causing them. Later, her father, who had climbed onto the platform beside Daya, would tell her that the noise was caused by Hans ramming the front end of his Jeep against the steel gate, trying to batter it down.

"Derek—*help* me! Let me *in!*" Hans half-stood with his hand on the steering wheel. "I have *no-where!*"

Derek couldn't speak. He could only watch as Hans dropped to the seat and made the engine roar. The car shot forward, its front bumper smashing against the gate again. One of the posts cracked, and the gate began to sag. The car leapt back.

"Papa!" Lila shouted.

Then Derek turned and saw her standing below in the rain next to the old palm-frond lean-to. He waved frantically, motioning her to stay back. Then, turning back to the road, he leaned over the top of the gate. *"No!"* he screamed at Hans. "I have my family here! *Go away!"*

Hans turned in his seat, and then, at the same time that Derek and Daya saw it, he caught sight of the approaching army van.

Now Lila was at the platform steps, her upturned face dripping with rain. "Papa, come back to the house!" she cried into the roaring sound from the other side of the gate. "I don't want to leave you here!"

Derek looked out along the road, past the Jeep with its tires whining and spinning in the mud, past the sheets of rain striking the road's surface. Two gray vans were speeding toward him now. He heard cracks of gunfire— soldiers in the vans shooting at Hans. The German stood holding his pistol out at arm's length. He fired first at the vans, then swiveled and pointed the gun at Derek at the top of the gate.

"You must let me *in!*"

"*No.*" Grabbing Daya's arm, Derek ducked toward the wooden steps. "I'm coming back, Lila!" he shouted at his daughter.

A roaring sound expanded in Lila's ears and ended with a crash. The gate rocked toward her, then wobbled back; so did the stairs where Daya and her father stood. The clatter of gunshots grew louder. She could see a strip of the road now between the edge of the gate and the broken post. A flash of red ripped through the rain, and Hans's Jeep came flying toward her.

Its battered front end struck the gate again with a horrible metallic explosion. The yellow-haired figure toppled forward over the windshield and dove onto the mud. Lila saw her father and Daya jump from the platform steps as the structure came crashing to the ground, boards flying everywhere.

Another vehicle was behind her now—the Land Rover. It skidded in the mud, its door opening. There was Richard and her mother. And there was her father, stumbling to his feet. And Hans was nearby, too, staggering in place, one arm raised in the air. The Jeep lay still, its hood giving off a gasp of smoke and black stench. Hans's pistol went off; the bullet clanged against the front end of an army van just outside the collapsed gate.

Then Hans was stumbling toward Lila, his half-red face clenched, his eyes burning. "I have a hostage!" he screamed, diving toward her. She jumped sideways. A wet hand gripped her ankle. She fell hard onto the mud. The hand held her like the jaws of an animal. Digging her fingers into the ground, she tried to pull away and kicked wildly. Her foot struck Hans's face, again and again.

"*You stop!*" Hans grunted, heaving his body over her.

"No!" Lila felt the heavy steel of the pistol against her neck. She inhaled Hans's stink—sweat, liquor, something else: terror. It was stronger than any fear she had of the pistol. "*No!*" she screamed again, squirming sideways.

A huge gray van turned into the drive, screeched to a halt beside the smashed gatepost. Lila saw Hans rise to his knees and point the pistol at the van. She heard no shot, only a click. She felt Hans's grip on her loosen. Now Richard and Sue were beside Hans, tugging at him, pummeling his back with their fists. Lila rolled away free. Hans stumbled to his feet.

Lila heard loud cracks at close range. Sitting, she saw soldiers beside the van, their rifles raised. Hans swayed in place, blood streaming from his bare shoulder. Then he was running from the rifles, slipping in the mud, staggering up the driveway. Nearly collapsing, he veered off down the side path—the false one with the narrowing fence of wire. He rushed on, the barbs tearing at his pants. Once, he whirled around, struggling to get free of the wire, but it seemed to claw at his trousers' legs, shredding them as he tugged his way along. Lila heard him groaning. More soldiers rushed toward the van.

"Lila, keep down!" Her father crawled along the ground toward her.

Rifles went off everywhere. The earth rippled near Lila's face. She saw Daya fall to the ground, his hand slapped against his stomach.

Then with a scream, Hans collapsed, his arms and torso held up only by the barbs in the wire. His head rose toward the gate, and for a moment, Lila saw him staring at her, pleading.

She was pushed flat to the ground as more bullets sprayed the air. An arm and shoulder covered her head—

her father's. She felt the reverberations of boots as the soldiers rushed past.

Richard and Mum were back with her now. Her mother, hair flattened with rain, stroked Lila's muddy face as if to see her more clearly. Richard knelt beside her, too, his hand resting on her shoulder. He pulled her father gently onto his side. Papa's arm was shiny with blood. His eyes were wide open.

"Lila!" He reached out toward her.

Lunging forward, she pressed her face into her father's chest.

COLORADO

2001

In her art class, Lila poked little holes along the top of a stretched canvas with the pointed end of her brush. Then she began pressing feathers and strings of beads into some of the openings. The other students watched her place the canvas not on an easel but on a windowsill, where sunbeams shone behind it and turned the holes to flashes of light. She stood back, stirring oils on her palette, staring hard at the blank white space which to her was an open window.

"A dream-catcher," a student said, pointing to the holes. They weren't such a mystery now.

*

Lila still remembered a smaller "dream-catcher" that had dangled from the rearview mirror of Richard's car. He'd told her what it was called on the day she arrived in America, when he and his wife, Raquel, met her at the Denver airport and drove her to their home in a small country town.

"But what *is* it?" she asked, pointing to the webbed loop of beads and feathers.

"Some folks think they're Indian talismans," Raquel said. "Other people say they're just handicraft things that old hippies borrowed from my people. I don't know, myself."

"It's beautiful." Lila reached out to touch the loop. Before her, it made a frame around the snowy mountains that would have been too vast to comprehend without it.

"Do they really catch dreams?" Lila asked.

Richard smiled at her. "If you believe it."

"You can save up your dreams and shake the catcher over your bed," Raquel said, "so you'll have beautiful pictures to keep you company in your sleep."

"And they're supposed to keep nightmares from getting into your room," Richard said

Lila glanced up at Raquel.

"Most nightmares, anyway," Raquel said. "You want one in your bedroom window, honey?"

Lila nodded. "Yes, please."

"We'll hang one up for you," Richard said.

Lila needed it. Some bad dreams haunted her sleep. She was homesick and missed her parents badly. She couldn't paint or even draw anything. When she thought of Sri Lanka, she ached. America amazed and appalled her; it was even bigger and noisier and more exciting than it looked in the few films she'd seen. And colder—all day, she wore two or three sweaters to keep out the chilly air; at night, her teeth chattered as she huddled under layers of blankets. The roadside restaurants—bright, rounded plastic buildings sparkling with neon—delighted her to look at, but they served meat hidden between round pieces of bread; the smell of cooked animal flesh sent her gagging out the door. Boxes on supermarket shelves screamed strange words. But the shops and public buildings smelled clean. The police didn't demand to look at your papers or poke you with rifle barrels; some people even asked policemen questions in the streets, though Lila never did. Girls dressed like film stars, showing their bare skin in halters and shorts; it was no wonder the boys teased them at school.

At first, Lila was the smallest girl in her class. The white students were polite, but many of them didn't really want to get to know her. Some seemed uneasy that her uncle had married an Indian. Most people were a little in awe of her because she was foreign. Only the Indian kids hung around after school to walk partway home with her. Many of them kept horses tied up among some trees near the school so they could ride them the rest of the way to their houses. Raquel gave Lila a palomino mare and taught her how to ride. Then Lila tied the horse in the grove, too. She fell in love with it, learning to brush and curry it for hours. She called it "*Sambhur,*" and told the Indians that the name meant "wild deer" in her home language.

"We used to see them where we lived," she said. "Also, I had a cat."

"What happened to it?" a boy asked.

"She was murdered." Lila looked away. "But she was old. She couldn't have come here." Lila didn't try to tell anyone at school about Daya, and how the last thing he'd said to her was that he promised to look for her cat.

At night, when Richard and Raquel were asleep, she sometimes remembered Daya and pressed her fists against her eyes. She hoped that the dream-catcher in her window would keep out demons, but it couldn't stop some of them from flying all the way from Sri Lanka. She heard them moving around her bed; when she tried to understand their words, a terrible huge silence welled up. It sucked away all the air in her room, making her gasp. Suddenly she exploded the emptiness with scream after scream. Raquel and Richard rushed into her room and sat beside her on the bed until she could breathe normally again.

Then she talked about what had happened on the day she had left the plantation, though Richard knew about it already, of course—the crack of rifle fire, and Hans hanging in the barbed wire with blood leaking down his bare chest, and Daya collapsed on the ground, wide-eyed, mud-splattered, motionless in the pouring rain.

She remembered Richard carrying her father to the Land Rover. In Papa's left arm, Lila learned later, were bullets that would have embedded themselves in her head if he hadn't thrown himself over her as the soldiers opened fire.

Richard laid Daya's body in the back of the car, then ran round to the driver's seat. He drove as fast as he could until he had to slam on the brakes at a roadblock. Soldiers surrounded the car with rifles bristling. For a while they considered letting Richard go but keeping Lila and her parents behind.

"No way!" Richard said, gripping the steering wheel with both hands.

"My husband has to go to the hospital!" Sue cried.

"We're neutral! We're innocent!" Derek shouted at the soldiers, even as one of them prodded his neck with a rifle barrel. "*Let my family go!*"

Canvas-backed trucks sped up the road. Lila heard gunshots from behind a bamboo fence. The soldiers at the roadblock rushed back to their van. Richard drove on, dodging military vehicles. Turning in her seat, Lila saw billows of black smoke rise from the trees beside the road.

Finally they were driving through the streets of Colombo. In a hospital courtyard, Lila saw several men lying on the grass with stumps of arms and legs in white bandages. She was afraid one of them would sit up and salute her, but they just lay still, staring into space, and she was ashamed of her fear. When Richard and Sue tried to get medical help for Derek, the police drove him off into the night. Three weeks later, Lila and Sue went to a courtroom where he was shackled to a wooden bench wearing old gray pajamas, his arm in a cast. He was charged with receiving undeclared funds from a foreign national and bribing a public official. One of his eyes was shut, the lid a dark purple that throbbed in the harsh fluorescent light. When he tried to smile over at Lila, she saw the wet red cracks in his lips and knew he had been badly beaten. She hated the blank-eyed government soldiers in the courtroom who pretended not to notice her father's face.

He was released on bail and allowed to live with Lila, Mum, and Richard in an aunt's house in Colombo while he began preparing his court case. Eventually, their attorney told the family that their plantation, among others, had been used by Tamil Tigers who had been gradually moving onto the grounds. The rebels had slipped into abandoned outbuildings and forced workers out of their houses, keeping them quiet with threats or with cash. Their funds filtered down from the Assistant Minister—the one who had visited Derek and other landowners in the area—in exchange for an agreement not to attack plantations in his constituency.

"I thought we were safe there," Lila said to Richard, after the lawyer left. She squinted up at him. "Was Papa...crazy? I mean, to give money to that politician?"

Richard shook his head. "He was desperate. Do you understand the difference?"

Lila bit her lip. "I think so...now."

The Tigers, Richard explained, had said they intended only to establish a base through which they could funnel supplies to their troops in the North. But after a while the Assistant Minister withheld funds, depositing them in European bank accounts for himself, and the agreement with the guerillas fell apart. Just after Lila and the family left the sanctuary, the Tigers set fire to several plantations. Within weeks, the government cleared the area of rebels during a campaign that left many civilians dead, most of them Tamils. Under wartime emergency laws, Derek's land was held as a militarized zone.

For months, Lila lived in Colombo helping her mother take care of her father. She wrote to Radha, hoping the school at Kaduwa would forward her letters to Canada. A letter finally arrived from Toronto: Radha's burns had slowly healed, she said, but her father was still too badly hurt to practice medicine. Nobody knew when he would recover. She liked her new school, though some of the students who were Tamils and Sinhalese got into violent fights in the car park after football matches.

Richard went back to Colorado to help run the tree nursery that he and Raquel had bought. He phoned Colombo often, his voice sounding far away. Papa's arm healed and his headaches gradually stopped, but each time he came back from a police interrogation he went into his room and lay on his bed for days with the curtains drawn. The court case dragged on.

Then in one of Richard's letters came an airline ticket for Lila to Colorado, USA.

*

Now it was Papa and Mum who sounded impossibly far away on the phone. They were sure to win the case, Papa said—next month…summer, they hoped…September for sure. She missed the plantation so badly! What had happened to it? Lila asked. Silence. We don't know, her mother said. We'll know more soon, her father said.

Eventually Lila stopped asking about home. It was, she thought, her phantom limb.

Still, she had a house to live in here in America, several cats almost as nice as Zalie, and even a horse that grazed out behind the trailer. Finally used to the weather, she went for long rides every day, and the snow was as beautiful on the mountain slopes as she'd once pictured it. She loved working with Richard and Raquel at the tree nursery. After a while, fewer demons flew into her dreams to wake her. On the phone, she told her parents about her new adventures: playing real softball, riding in a rodeo pageant, going to powwows where she and Richard watched Raquel dance in beautiful feathered dresses. Lila didn't mention any pictures to her parents; she still couldn't draw or paint, though her room was full of new art supplies.

One day Raquel asked Lila to make a portrait of her wearing her feathered dance clothes.

"I don't know," Lila said, looking down at her hands.

She mixed some oil paints but the brush felt like a stiff, cold snake in her fingers, about to wake and wriggle uncontrollably. Richard stood beside her easel, talking slowly. He played a tape from one of the powwows.

"Does the drumming remind you of the ceremony at the plantation?" he asked.

"A little." Lila stared at the canvas.

"How long do I have to sit here like a big bird?" Raquel asked.

Lila began to paint. First the colors—yellow, red, blue, silver. Then Raquel's shape, her dark face and big, brown eyes, her beautiful woven braid. When the canvas was finished, Richard hung it in the living room beside the window.

Soon Lila worked every day, and kept a sketchbook with her everywhere. Her pictures took the place of all the ones she'd left behind in Sri Lanka, she said. But she still couldn't bring herself to draw scenes of Sri Lanka or the plantation.

Next spring, Lila's mother was no longer a voice on the telephone or a presence she cried out for when she woke in the night. She was here in Colorado, running across the carpet in the airport; her hair was flying, her arms out to hold Lila in her strong grip. Papa had finally been cleared of the charges against him; he would come as soon as he could get some money from his family and secure the plantation. It took a while for Lila to get to know her mother again; they had both changed so much. Sue actually looked a little younger and less tired. She didn't understand all the new things in America—malls, video games, computers. Sometimes she asked Lila the kinds of questions a kid would ask a mother. Lila hardly ever asked anyone kid-questions any longer; she felt like the oldest student in her class.

On a television broadcast one night, she saw pictures of Colombo and looked for her father, but all the scenes were in a part of the city far from where he was staying. Richard and Raquel and Mum gathered around when Lila called out to them. The screen showed people staggering through rubble in the streets. Scenes were lit by the flickering orange light of flames in collapsed building. Sirens screamed. Bodies covered in blankets were loaded into the back of vans. One of the dead men had been the prime minister's bodyguard, the announcer said. A suicide bomber had tried to blow up the prime minister as she made a campaign speech. A few moments later, Chandrika Kumaratunga herself appeared on the screen. One of her eyes was covered with a bulging white bandage, and red scrape-marks shone on her ashen cheeks.

"We will *never* let these terrorists destroy democracy...*never!*" She shouted—first in English, and then, with a strange, scratchy tone, in Sinhala and in Tamil.

The sound of her home languages was what made Lila burst out in tears. She'd used the languages in her head to hold imaginary conversations with her old schoolmates, but she hadn't heard anyone speak them aloud for more than two years. Now she could suddenly hear all the shuddering nuances of desperation in Chandrika's voice.

Sue wrapped her arms around her and Richard held her hand, but Lila couldn't stop sobbing. Finally Raquel brought a cool, wet towel for her face and she was able to catch her breath. The television screen was blank now, but it still seemed tinted with reflections of orange flames.

"How can people do—do those—" She couldn't finish.

The trailer was silent. She felt her mother's breath close to her cheek. But Chandrika's voice echoed from the shadows behind the set.

"I don't understand—" she tried again.

"None of us really do," Richard said quietly. "You're in good company."

"You're safe now," Sue told Lila. "No terrorists can come here...."

She went silent as Raquel let out a soft groan. "What you saw—" Raquel glanced at the television, and then stared far beyond it. "Things like that happened to my people years ago, over and over." Raquel took the towel from Lila's hand and wiped her own face. "But we survived it all. Just barely, sometimes. But we did. And we can do it again if we have to."

Lila looked at Raquel, then at her mother and Richard. Her mother loosened her grip on her. Richard nodded. "All right," she said. Then she said it again in Sinhala and Tamil. Her words sounded scratchy to her but she could believe them, barely.

The next morning, she painted a big landscape of Sri Lanka in art class. It was the canvas with the holes along the top. When she'd finished, they looked like stars shining in daylight. The picture was of no specific place, she told the students, just the country. The teacher had once pointed it out on a wall map; to them it was just a teardrop-shaped island floating in the ocean far away somewhere in Asia. They stared at the painting, not knowing what to say. There were greens that made you feel wonderfully cool and other greens that gave you a shivery sensation as if you were looking into a bowl of vipers. There were purples that, spreading over a sky, looked like velvet cloth you wanted to stroke; other purples tinted shadows and resembled bruises you couldn't stand to touch. You could almost hear flocks of yellow birds as they swooped into storm clouds that became so dark they seemed to growl. Tranquil water buffaloes waded in rivers where the current ran blue and then turned dark red. Some shades of orange gave off the scent of blossoms; other shades turned flowers into mouthfuls of flames. The landscape looked like a big garden, pristine and elegant, until you saw a soldier lying along a tree branch or a boar-faced creature with bloody tusks squatting behind a bougainvillea bush.

*

Almost a year later her father arrived. At the airport he looked thin, his hair clipped short and gray, his beard shaved off.

"You've grown so big here!" he said as he hugged Lila. "Do you remember me?"

"Of course, Papa!" she cried, squeezing him back. She didn't say how much smaller he seemed.

For many months, Derek wrote to his attorneys who were trying to force the government in Colombo to give back his plantation. "Are the workers all right?" he demanded. "Who's tending the gardens?—irrigating the paddy fields?—taking care of the buffaloes?" It was hard for Lila to think about these problems; she had so much to do at school and the nursery. Finally Derek stopped writing letters, and no more letters arrived from the lawyers. He helped in the nursery when it expanded, and Sue found a job in the town. Eventually Lila's parents rented a house for themselves and Lila. Her father began a garden, experimenting with new plant breeds he ordered from the state university.

Then one day, when Lila arrived home from school, she found her parents and Richard sitting around the kitchen table. They were looking through photographs of the plantation that the attorneys had mailed from Sri Lanka. Many of the photos were blurred, tilted, with objects so off-center they seemed to be tottering off the edge of the paper.

They hardly reminded Lila of a place where she'd once lived. Hillsides where rubber trees had grown now bristled with stumps; the land looked scorched everywhere. She saw kitchen walls blackened with smoke, the floor empty where the stove had been ripped out, the taps gone except for two pipes protruding from the wall. (But there—the coconut scraper was still attached to the counter, its handle raised as if someone were about to start turning it.) The sitting room was a roofless place with collapsed beams. Lila looked in vain for playing cards. Two entire walls of the room were expanses of air. (But in a patch of weeds growing from a crack in the floor were some charred art books whose pictures she knew by heart.) Her room's walls were still standing, though all the furniture was gone and the roof was caved in. (But her portrait of the Buddha was still taped up near the window; his calm, half-closed eyes gazed down, undisturbed by the rubble around him.) She handed the photos to her parents.

"Do you want to keep them?" Richard asked her.

"I think I'll make my own pictures," Lila said.

That was how she wanted to go back home now. She was ready to paint the house and the cricket pitch, the gardens and paths, the white cranes flying low pitch the paddy fields and the deer running through the trees near the bamboo wall. The real sanctuary, thanks to her mother and father and Richard, was in her memory. Now she would be able to smell the land's greenness again. She could hear the palm fronds crackling in the rain. She would feel the place's warmth surround her like a breath and know that it would be there when she needed it.